Confessions of a Chihuahua: Memoir of An Amazing Dog

As told to
Anne Compton

Praise for *Confessions of a Chihuahua*

A note from Khaki (the dog whose picture on the cover made you say aww even though you hadn't planned on it):

I know this review stuff is usually saved for the back cover, but I'm so proud of my story that I decided to put them right here in the front. I just know it will fire you up to read the rest.

"I couldn't wait to put this book down."
    The Puppy Times

"...a level of narcissism typically reserved for soon to be beheaded royalty."
    Muzzle & Tail Magazine

"This book is crammed full of incomparable drivel."
    Brutus Smythe, author of Canine History

"Meh."
    Tony, Neighborhood Watch captain

"My life is now complete. I truly hope this dog doesn't understand sarcasm."
Lisa, semi-professional editor

Getting ahead of the game

I always knew that I would be famous one day, felt it down deep in my paws. How things have come about though, is not what I expected. I always thought...we'll get to that later. Anyway, out with Mama in the big store with the concrete floor was not the time or place I had expected for my life to have a major turning point.

It was a pretty Saturday morning, and Mama took me with her to do some shopping. We walked all through that store, making quick stops every once in a while when Mama got distracted by something pretty. Finally we arrived in the back of the store where we stopped and were looking at the dishwashers (Mama really values my opinion), when I happened to look over my shoulder. I noticed a teenager in a striped beanie and ripped jeans messing with his phone down the aisle from us. My heart started going double time when I noticed that the bubble eye in the phone's top corner was aimed right at me.

What an invasion of privacy! He hadn't even bothered to ask permission to gawk at me like that.

I felt used, and I could've spit nails. Well, I'm nothing if not poised, so I did my best to stay under control. I didn't make a sound because I didn't want to draw attention, but you better believe I stared beanie boy down. When he finally had the guts to make eye contact with me, he quickly stabbed his finger at the phone a couple times and stuffed it in his pocket. Then he started whistling like cartoon characters do when they want to look like they have no idea what's going on. Seriously. You could see the guilt all over his zit covered face.

The evidence was just too much. He had taken my picture. And you know teenagers, it would be online within the hour, and then just like that, I would be Miss viral Khaki. Then pretty soon the paparazzi would be camping outside my house, trying to flatten themselves into the ditch across the street, or climbing up into the neighbor's tree, swapping out camera lenses until they finally managed to catch me in a compromising position in the backyard. If you don't know what I'm talking about, ask someone who says y'all, I know you know at least one, what shoo-shoo is. A real lady such as yours truly doesn't talk about such things.

Anyway, the point is that this is not even a tiny bit acceptable to me. Humiliation is surely coming if I don't make the first move. So I'll take the high road and be the one

to make that first move without calling out the beanie wearing hooligan who forced me into this. I couldn't if I wanted to. I don't know his name. And let's be honest, there are a lot of beanie wearing hooligans in this world.
I will write the truth. (With Mama's help, of course. I hate to admit it, but I'm not fluent in English. I can understand what someone says to me, but I can't speak, read, or write a lick. My Dogspeak, though, is excellent. Ask any dog in the southeast.) I'll give all my history, pull every tiny skeleton out of my tasteful closet. Then, no matter what might be said or written about me later on, the <u>actual</u> facts will already exist in the world for anyone willing to put in a little

effort and look for them. I'm defending myself before the trial, you might say. It's really all I can do.

I'm grateful that Mama is willing to help me with this. If she didn't, I don't know what I would do. Even though she doesn't know Dogspeak, we have made our own kind of language. We talk to each other very well, as a lot of dogs do with their person. So to write this book, we will talk all of it through together. Mama will do the translating as we go along, being careful to fully express every one of my ideas and thoughts. There might even be a few spots where you can tell we're working things out between us. I think that in the end, the effort will be worthwhile for all of us... me, Mama, and you, my lovely readers.

When I have completed this, I will again have peace. Only then will I be able to sleep at night, and probably also some in the morning and afternoon. I hate to admit it, but the emotional turmoil and lack of beauty sleep is starting to take its toll on me. Yesterday, I thought I saw a bag starting to form under my left eye.

Pupdom

Let me start this tail (See what I did there? I'm so clever.) by exposing to the world my biggest shame. I'm not going to hold back. If I did, how could I expect anyone to take me seriously and believe what I do write? So here is the ugly truth: I come from a broken home.

My mother was a very pretty petite Boston Terrier named Pthwee. She came from a long line of prized lap dogs belonging to the rich and famous, or at least pretty well off and not anonymous. She had silky fur, a regal nose, and slender ankles like a thoroughbred. It seems that she was not pretty enough, or that my father was off in the head, because he left her with a young litter when a big eyed Yorkie sashayed past the yard. At least that's the story.

He was a rat faced Chihuahua with a stubby tail, and being with him meant that my mother had to move to a middle class neighborhood and adjust to a less refined lifestyle than she was used to. I have no idea what she saw in him. Maybe he had money at some point. I would hate to think of my mother as possibly being a gold digger, but who knows? Sometimes family secrets are actually secrets and not just forgotten information. In that case, it's best to let sleeping dogs lie. I don't even remember my father's name. Anyway, he spends very little time in my life and story, so we'll just gloss right over him.

If you've been paying attention, you will have gathered that I'm part Boston Terrier and at most 50% Chihuahua. So why claim the genetics of the parent I don't even like? *Confessions of a Chihuahua* has a nice sound to it, that's mostly why I chose the title. I like it when words start the same way. The fifty cent word for that is alliteration, Mama says. Also, I chose it for the sake of marketing. And while I might not be the tiny shaking dog you expect, I look much better with my less compact body paired with the cute and unmistakable Chihuahua apple head. I figured anyone with eyes that work could tell that I'm part Chihuahua. So big deal, I'm not a purebred. "Mutt" or not, I'm still a queen. As solid proof, God gave me a built in tiara. You saw my picture on the cover, right? Come on, you know that diamond on my forehead was no mistake.

My mother named me Hoowpha. That's probably not exact, because direct translation from Dogspeak to English is tough. The best way I can describe it is that it sounds kind of like the word I heard someone in a movie say once when he slurped down a fizzy drink too fast.

Let me explain dog names here. I know Hoowpha and Khaki sound nothing alike, and that's because dogs have different kinds of names. Our parents, sometimes the entire pack, but usually just the parents, give us a Dogspeak name at about one week old. Since people don't know Dogspeak, when a dog is loved by a person and given a new name, it's in a different language. At that point, not only people but also dogs outside the immediate family start using the new name. Close family, I think the word here is actually nuclear, will keep using the Dogspeak name. So as an example, my third cousin Guarng became Cookie to me when he was taken in and renamed by a human family, but I will always call my siblings by their Dogspeak names.

I have three sisters and two brothers. We are my mother's first and maybe only litter. I don't know much about her life before she moved to the yard where I grew up. She kept that information to herself, and as her pup, it's important that I respect that.

Poor Rught is the runt, and ugly too, bless him. He must have done something wrong with the genes he was given, because the rest of the litter is gorgeous. He was what almost kept me from leaving home, because I knew that seeing my face every day gave him hope that even an ugly pup could become a beautiful swan.

Browrargh, my other brother, is two minutes older than me, and never let me forget it. He seemed to think his extra two minutes of age meant he was my boss, and he was always trying to make me do things for him like find the piece of rope he liked to play with. I knew good and well that thing was usually balled up in a mud puddle somewhere. There are few things I like less than getting dirty. And of course it wasn't fair that he expected me to do his work. I had no problem telling him he shouldn't lose his stupid rope. I also usually added that since he was losing things, he should lose the lazy and go get the rope himself. Sometimes after a good telling off, he would lower his eyes and give me a nice little nuzzle behind one of my ears. I would forgive him instantly, because I just couldn't stay mad at the big lovable goof. There was a lot of tension in our relationship, but we loved each other.

Big sis, Thwerpa was an excellent liar. She could get us girls off the hook for anything, and we put her skill to the test quite a few times. Once she convinced our father (back when he still loved us and stayed home) that we hadn't left the yard, but that he had fallen asleep and dreamed it. It was a work of genius. We had been gone for hours, gorging ourselves on bits of leftover donuts we found on the pavement near the bakery half a mile away. Our father bought every word Thwerpa said, probably because he wasn't so innocent himself, and none of us girls were pulled by the scruff to timeout.

Wurfy, the second oldest sister, is a full fledged Chihuahua at heart and a master heel nipper. She could get any of us pups, and even surprised our mother sometimes. In general, her nipping was annoying, but she did save our hides once when a big nasty possum came creeping around. Her ears popped up straight as could be. Then off she ran like her tail was on fire, and nipped right up on him. The dumb thing forgot to play dead when she nipped, and took off toward the woods running just as ugly as you would expect a possum to run. We all howled with laughter, and Wurfy got a little extra snuggle time with our mother that night.

My favorite sibling though, is my sister Aarfah, because she's most like me. Sometimes we would stay up almost all night woofing it up, talking about how weird our brothers smelled. We practiced etiquette together, learning in which direction to eat from a short bowl or a tall bowl. We spent many afternoons walking around balancing magnolia leaves on our heads, working to improve our posture. I loved to sneak up beside her while she was focusing on keeping the leaf still and blow it off her head. She would get furious and bare her little white teeth at me, but only for a second. Aarfah did the same thing to me every chance she got. Really, we were best friends. We had fun, for sure. We could almost read each other's mind, and so we always knew what the other needed.   Twice the fun and half the problems.

Ordinarily I would feel jealous of such a wonderful pup like Aarfah, but she is just a smidge less cute than me. You know every girl wants to be the pretty one, though most of us would never admit it. The ones who can't be the pretty one want to be the smart one or the funny one. We all just have to be special in some way, and I think that's as it should be. Anyway, Aarfah has a diamond on her forehead too, but it's not quite as well defined and nicely shaped as mine. Also, both of her ears stick straight up. My left ear sticks straight up, but the right sticks mostly up, with the tip flopping over just a bit. Cuter than unicorn snot, I'm told. So because I come out the winner in those two areas, she was no threat to me, and on top of that, she was supportive of my dreams.

Speaking of, and this is very important to my story, my big dream was to become a singer. No, not just a singer, a singer songwriter star. I have the voice, the smarts, the look, the attitude. I knew that Podunkville (That's the name I use for where I grew up. I'm not sure what people call it.) couldn't contain me. I was meant for a national if not global stage.

I spent hours every day composing and perfecting new songs. I tried out dance moves, practiced cute stances, and even experimented with facial expressions. I'm very dedicated to my craft, and I'm happy to say that each song I created went over well. They were so good that they brought tears to the eyes of my family when I sang them. Sometimes my mother would totally break down and blubber cry with pride. When I saw everyone's reaction to my work, I couldn't help but puff out my cute little chest just a bit more as I sang louder.

All my success at home left me restless, wanting to share my gems with the public. Still wet behind the ears, I just didn't know how to go about pursuing stardom. I couldn't stand the idea of an innocent newbie like myself being taken advantage of, working too hard for too little, that kind of thing. There were just so many things I didn't understand yet. But I also knew that my gift had to be shared. It's wrong to keep a gift to yourself. Everyone deserves to hear some goodness, after all. I would not give up, no matter how difficult the journey became. The timing was just not right yet. I would have to be patient while I listened, watched, and learned. This was the key to real success.

One night, the dogstar aligned, and my grand plan was hatched. It had just been a normal day, but that night goes down in Khaki history. My mother was watching some cheesy reality show through the neighbor's window, and I decided to join her for some girl bonding time. When the weatherman did a little segment between commercials, he mentioned Nashville and pointed to it on the weather map. That was when the sky parted and inspiration struck.

Suddenly I knew that I had to get to Nashville. That is the place where stars are made, and of course I was for sure an unmade star. Now I know what you're thinking, that Nashville is for country music, but let me tell you how wrong you are. Sure, they do a lot of country in Nashville, and they do it well, but the scene has expanded. Personally, (Maybe it should be dogally?) I have no problem with country music. I think some of it is great. But my short legs just can't pull off cowgirl boots. Those are best left to greyhounds. I have more eclectic taste anyway.

Since the weatherman had pointed to Nashville, and it was apparently on the same map as Podunkville, I knew it couldn't be too far away, at least not on the other side of the world. Now how to get there?

Remembering some episodes of Dateline I had seen a while back, I figured that hitchhiking was a good way to cover all that ground, especially since I didn't have any money. Dogs never have money. We are forced to get by on our looks and charm, and thankfully, I'm blessed with both. It seems that hitchhikers always have a bag or suitcase, but I couldn't for the life of me figure out how I was going to carry one unless I suddenly sprouted thumbs. It looked like my only option was a collar. Shudder. I kind of hated myself for it, but I went to the far end of the doghouse and dug up my old collar. I had buried it a long time ago because I hated it and didn't want to ever see it again.

So once it was on, I went on the search for anything I might need on my trip. When I accidentally found a nice bone one of my brothers might or might not have been saving for a rainy day, I patiently wiggled myself into a downward facing dog position until I managed to slide it under the collar. That would just have to be enough luggage. If I added anything else, I wouldn't be able to walk comfortably. I had no doubt I could live off the fat of the land if necessary, but surely a sweet person would rescue this damsel in distress right away and whisk me off to Nashville where all my wildest dreams would come true.

I was so excited by my plan that I had to force myself not to blurt everything out. I knew my mother wouldn't approve, so I spent hours struggling to look calm and like there wasn't a brilliant idea floating in my brain. I also spent a lot of time in a leaf pile so nobody would notice that I was wearing the hated collar. If someone had seen it, my plan would have died right there.

I barely managed it, but I waited until everyone had piled up together and fallen asleep. Everyone except my father, that is, since he had already left us for that brazen

Yorkie. At least with me gone, our mother would have one less pup to take care of. And when I made it big, I would buy a great big house for us all (again, except my father) to share. My leaving might cause a little sadness for now, but soon it would all be worthwhile.

I walked quietly out of the yard, doing my best not to step on any twigs. If I could have slithered out of there like a worm, I would have. Without meaning to, I was holding my breath. I was terrified of being caught and forced to stay home. As I made it past the yard, breathing came a little easier. Smiling at the thought of my success, I made my way to a big road, and waited for my ride to appear.

This is when I discovered that I'm scared of moving cars. I don't mind them when they're sitting in the driveway, I even like to ride in them sometimes. But to be honest, watching tires zoom past my face really freaked me out. I'm not saying this happened, but yelling and running for dear life would have been a sane reaction to what I experienced out there.

My next instinct was to follow the railroad tracks. They always lead to big cities, right? The best part of this idea was that there are no cars driving on the tracks. Actually, there's almost nothing going on by railroad tracks. There would be no one around to bother me. This also meant no one to talk to, but I decided that safety was more important than having friends. At least for now. When I got to Nashville and needed to make connections for my career's sake, it would be a different story. It might take me a long time to make it all the way there, on paw all by myself, but I knew that I could...would do it.

Doing time

I thought a producer had heard of my plight and sent a limo for me when I saw headlights coming toward me about twenty minutes later. I was sadly mistaken since it turns out that I was picked up, not by a chauffeur, but a cop. The cop scooped me up and dropped me in the back of a muddy truck. Soon I found that instead of perching myself in a plush seat surrounded by tasty snacks, I would have to ride standing, separated from the cop by some sturdy wire mesh. The roads around Podunkville aren't the smoothest, but I think that truck must have had no shocks at all. The ride was terribly bumpy, and it felt like some of my parts were shaken from their original positions. I started to get carsick. I shouldn't have worried about feeling like I might make a mess, being picked up without cause and all, but my sense of good manners made me nervous about it anyway. But only a tiny bit. Thankfully the ride was just a few minutes, or things in the back could have gotten really ugly if you know what I mean.

Unfortunately that short ride meant I was soon in jail. The cop, without a word, put me into an empty cell. Straight into solitary confinement, and I hadn't even put up a struggle. And what happened to Miranda rights? This all seemed very unprofessional, but I immediately decided that I would have to adjust to my situation. Raising a fuss would probably only make things worse.

The sound of other dogs echoed all around me, but try as I might, I couldn't see them. I think I spent four days in solitary. Time kind of runs together in a cell with artificial light. I guess I should be grateful that I didn't spend all that time in the dark. That would have been terrible. At least I had good company, and also lots of time to get myself under control. Anyway, the kibble was decent, and there was always a bowl full of clean water. I never got cold either, which is good, because I'm pretty delicate that way. Nobody ever told me why I was in jail. In fact, all I heard was a "Here you go" when food was brought to my cell, and the barking that probably came from some far away place. There was no due process at all: no questioning, no trial, but my best guess is that either I was arrested by mistake or that running away from home is against the law. There was little to do but sleep and worry, and I did plenty of both.

One morning, I woke up to someone talking to me. It took me a while to understand what was happening, because the name I kept hearing wasn't my name. The freckled, thick lipped girl standing outside my cell, the guard I guess, kept calling me Anna. I figured it was a case of mistaken identity, but I decided to go along with it until I could find a way to clear things up. Just how was a beautiful pup to get a lawyer? I hadn't been offered my rightful phone call, and even so I didn't know any phone numbers except 911. I didn't think that would do me any good from jail anyway. Up until that time, I had always relied on face to face talks to get what I needed, and it's still my favorite way to communicate. It helps that I have a great face. The problem here was that the girl and I seemed to be in different worlds. What she told me made no sense, and I don't think she could understand me at all.

After the guard talked to me a little, she grabbed me and took me out to the exercise yard. I'm not a fan of exercise, but at that point, I was willing to go anywhere that wasn't a tiny cell. I was so excited when I turned around and saw other dogs in the yard too! I'm actually not all that social, so I wasn't especially happy about the company, but maybe this meant that I was out of solitary now. After a good bit of sniffing around to get my bearings, I started to see some people coming in and out of the yard. They would walk around and look at all the dogs for a while, and then leave. Nobody stayed very long. This happened for a couple of hours before I spotted someone special.

She had curly hair and big dark eyes. Almost, but not quite, as nice as mine. I had seen my eyes once reflected in my water bowl and had been impressed by their perfect size and shape. Somehow I knew that she was a good person, and what's more, she was *my* person. It was one of those happy moments when your eyes pop out of the sockets and big hearts dance and swim around your head. She looked around the yard at all the dogs for a few minutes, then went over to a low retaining wall and sat down on it. It had been a rough few days for me, but now I saw my chance. Immediately, I snatched it. I walked over to her, and hopped up on the retaining wall right next to her. I sat down, then leaned over a little so our sides were touching. I knew I was in when she reached over and started to smooth my fur gently. Her hands felt soft and safe, and I felt so calm that I almost fell asleep. This was perfect.

She left, though, when a man outside the fence called to her. I couldn't even enjoy my first night out of solitary because I was worried sick that she might not come back for me. She was my only hope. Oh, I was sure I could work some magic and get someone to bail me out if I had to, but I had my heart set on her. My mind was uneasy, and I just couldn't get myself comfortable no matter what I tried. The thought came to me that I should scratch a poem about my inner turmoil on the cell wall, but I didn't want to ruin my nails. I would need to keep up my neat appearance just in case my person did come back to rescue me. She just had to. I pawed at the ratty blanket lining the cell much more than I normally would, trying to make it just right so I could get a little rest. It didn't matter. I was like the princess and the pea that night.

To my relief, she did come back the next day, but this time with the man and a dog. She came over to me in the yard and brought the crew with her. I greeted them with my sweetest puppy dog eyes, turning just so to let the sun make them sparkle.

Then it was on to winning my person over, because I just knew that if she wanted me, it didn't really matter what the man and dog thought. The goofy yet annoyed look on the dog's face let me know that she was not excited about the idea of having competition at home. Well, Peanut (that is her name) would just have to live with it. I quickly focused my attention on my person.

I smiled to let her see the perfect little teeth that would never tear up her shoes. I stretched a couple of times to let her see my nice muscles and thin waist. I held out a paw to let her see my delicate neat nails. For the big finish, I gave her a dainty lick on the hand to prove my undying affection. I had done my best. If I wasn't in now, there was no hope for me.

She looked thoughtful, and then asked the guard if I could go up and down stairs without any problems. She worried that my short legs wouldn't be able to make it without help. I laughed to myself, and then easily walked up and down a set of stairs the freckled thick lipped guard led me to. I was as prim and proper as I could be, promising without words that I was worth it. That seemed to seal the deal. Pretty soon, a bright green tag was placed around my neck. It meant that I was on the list to be bailed out!

The next day was the day before I was set to be released, and the jail threw me a party. My inner charm had won everyone over, canine and human, despite the fact that I kept to myself as much as I could. The cats down the hall don't count, they are impossible to charm.

My party must have been a good one, too, because I don't really remember much about it. According to the movies, the best parties leave you with no memories, so I guess mine would rate just shy of an A+. I do remember being carried into a room full of shiny things, and then put on a very cold and slippery dance floor. My usual practice is to make a big entrance to a party, but this time I was the first dog to arrive.

The next thing I knew, I woke up sore, with a lampshade on my head and a brand new tattoo. I must not have been thinking straight about the choice of tattoo, because I would never have decided to put a green circle on my belly if I had been in my right mind. A diamond or heart is more my taste, and placed on my hip or ear to be shown off to best effect. Oh well, what can you expect from a prison tattoo?

Day one drama

Let me start by saying that the day I was bailed out of jail was the best day of my life. Any strange behavior on my part was due to my state of being emotionally and physically overwhelmed. I think I actually had the vapors.

I woke up that morning still a little woozy from the party of a couple of days before. I had thought that I would be let out on bail right after the party, but every time the guard came by, it was for a different reason. By the morning of what would turn out to be my best day ever, I was starting to lose hope. Had I been wrong in thinking the party was for my release? Was it just some cruel joke to mess with my mind? Add those thoughts to my drowsiness, and you can see that I was in a fine state. I had been trying ever since noticing the lampshade on my head to get it off, but I had not been successful. Mostly, I wound up banging the lampshade on something, but instead of working it loose, my attempts just pushed the lampshade down into my shoulders. So when the guard came and took it off for me, I was happily surprised.

I ran around a little bit, and flicked my head around just to feel the increased range of movement.

Then she picked me up and took me to a big room where I saw my new people (I would soon come to call them Mama and The Backup) in the far corner. Excitement and hope flooded back into my heart at that second. Maybe I would make it out of there after all! Mama grinned at me, walked across the room, and handed over my bail money to the secretary. The guard gave me to Mama, and she hugged me. I was in a state of shock. After all the false hope, was this actually happening? Was I really going free now? And although I knew she was <u>my</u> person, I didn't know her very well, so it's possible that I wasn't quite as affectionate as I could have been. Instead of hugging her back and wagging my tail, I stared at her with my bewildered eyes, and didn't say a word. If I had been in my right mind, I could have said something special like from a movie script, but that didn't happen. I'm embarrassed by that fact.

The guard asked Mama what my name was going to be. I had been called Anna in the klink, but obviously that wouldn't work, because I heard the guard call Mama by a human name, Anne. Of course my name would have to change, it was too similar to hers, and would bring up bad memories of a dark time in my life. Besides,

Anna wasn't my name. As I mentioned earlier, my mother had named me Hoowpha.

Mama said that she had thought long and hard about it, and I would now be called Khaki, because most of my fur is that color. I kind of liked the sound of that. It's cute, but still I wasn't totally sold on it. Partly because I wanted some control over things, I mulled it over, and weeks later I approached Mama with my own idea. I wanted to change my name to A. Dora Bull, Dora for short. She laughed and said that name would only possibly work for a boy cow. Whatever that means. Anyway, really special people only need one name. Elvis.

Pelé. Aretha. So I guess I only need one, too.

I've caught The Backup a few times introducing me to his friends this way, "This is Khaki, like the pants." I am not amused by this, but he is. I always give him a not so subtle side eye to show him how I feel about that comparison, but he never notices. Anyway, sorry about that rabbit hole. It's just a small annoyance, really.

So after my bail had been paid, and Mama got a copy of my identification papers featuring my brand new name, we got in the car and left the jail. I was really happy and excited, but also a little nervous. I was starting a new life.

Everything was new to me, and I wasn't sure how I should act. After a few minutes, we parked in a huge parking lot, and Mama carried me into a big store. I relaxed in her arms while she and The Backup talked about which leash I should have. Bling or no bling? Obviously they didn't know me yet. Then I heard one of them say a terrible word: collar.

Now, I had just had the lampshade removed an hour ago, and I couldn't stand even the tiniest possibility of being yanked around by my neck, so I went into public meltdown mode, level overdrive. I crawled up Mama's shoulder and started pawing her hair down over her eyes while I tried to find an exit plan.

When The Backup tried to grab me, I jumped onto Mama's back and then to the floor where I wiggled under the shelf so fast no one could catch me. The Backup froze for a minute but then doubled over, laughing at me or Mama, I'm not sure which. As soon as Mama got enough hair out of her eyes to see, she took off and ran around the aisle, got down on the floor behind the shelf and tried to pull me out the back side. She couldn't reach me, and just to be sure, I curled into a ball in the center of the shelf where it would be hard for anyone to reach me. She yelled at The Backup to help her, but I'm not sure he heard because he was still cracking up. It was a chaotic scene with me balled up under the shelf,

Mama wriggling around on the floor trying to stretch a couple of extra inches, and The Backup laughing his donkey laugh with his hands on his knees. Somebody heard something, though, because a worker showed up to help. I knew because I saw a pair of sneakers walk over and stop right in front of me.

Between the three of them, especially if The Backup started to function, I didn't stand a chance. I soon wound up back in Mama's arms with a collar around my neck. All my scowling and fussing changed nothing. Mama didn't risk putting me on the ground, she continued to carry me. And that blasted collar went out the door with us.

Going to my new home and getting used to everything else was a breeze. In no time I knew all the great viewing spots in the house and the best places in the yard to take a nap in the sun. Peanut, who hadn't bothered to come along to bail me out, wasn't all that hard to tolerate. We got along, more or less, from the start.

You will find this hard to believe, but I can hold a grudge. There was one thing I was still unhappy with, and I wouldn't let it go. I kept making my feelings about the collar well known. Within a week Mama saw how nicely I walked beside her, whether in the yard or out in the neighborhood. This made her think, and she started to do a little research to see if I had a history of some phobia or trauma. Maybe I did have something going on in the way of phobias or trauma. I was happy with my new life, but there was something, I'm not sure what, that hadn't quite settled.

When Mama gets after something, she doesn't quit. So she kept up her research for some time. After reading online about small dogs' fragile windpipes (I might have accidentally stepped on the enter key to make sure she found what looked like a good article), she soon came home with a harness for me. I'm glad to report that I haven't been near a collar since.

Busting out

There is something I'm not proud of that I'm going to share with you now. Over the first few weeks that I spent in my new home, I left at least three times. Why on earth would I mess things up when I had it made? I was so insecure, but I've grown as a dog since then. Oh, it hurts my heart to talk about this, but I can't leave anything hidden. Suck it up, buttercup...I mean Khaki.

There are two doggy doors at home, one that opens onto the deck, where there are stairs leading down to the back yard, and the other opens straight onto the back yard. I learned early on that the deck is a nice place to relax because it can get toasty warm in the sun, and I spent a lot of time out there. (Still do.) I soon noticed that between the back deck and the carport there is a little half wall. Past that wall is a straight shot into the front yard. Now, I've got some hops in these short and shapely legs, and I used every bit of them to jump that wall three times.

I wasn't trying to do anything wrong, but when Mama and The Backup were both gone, I would get sad and lonely. I wondered if they were going to come back, and was terrified that they wouldn't. I never intended to run away, I just wanted to find them.

The first two times I never even made it out of the yard. They came home soon after my escapes to find me sniffing around the azaleas in front of the house. I do like a good sniff of azalea in the early afternoon. It was the third time that the consequences of my escape became very real and very scary.

I had hopped the half wall and finished sniffing the azaleas. I looked around, expecting to see the car coming down the road, but no

Mama, no car, no anything. Not even The Backup was around. That's when I got worried, because I was all alone. Peanut was in the house or in the back yard behind the fence, so I didn't even have her silly company. I flopped down in the grass to think and worry a little, when an amazing idea came to me. Our neighbor Mara liked me, and if I went to her porch, she would take care of me until somebody came home. Then I would be rescued, and all would again be right with the world.

So that's what I did. I walked across the yard to her porch, and sat myself down right in front of the door. She liked to keep her front door open with only the glass storm door closed, so her dog saw me immediately, and started whining for her attention. After telling Buster, that's her dog's name, to hush a couple of times, she gave in and decided to see what the problem was. Well, there I sat, all cute and pitiful. She took me inside like I knew she would, and gave me some nice cold water and a treat that tasted like peanut butter. When she noticed that Mama and the Backup were pulling the car into our driveway a few minutes later, she took me to them.

I'll never forget the look on Mama's face when the neighbor handed me to her. She looked like her heart broke and then all the pieces exploded. This was all my fault, and I was immediately ashamed. I almost cried, but that didn't seem like the right thing to do. So I just hung my head, tucked my tail, and gave her hand a little lick to say I was sorry. I should have known that they would come back. They had never done anything to make me think otherwise, but as I've since learned from my therapist, a sweet miniature Poodle, fear isn't rational.

I didn't get in trouble for what I had done. I almost wish I had, because that would have been easier on me. Instead, that weekend Mama and The Backup built a big planter box and filled it with tall grass. Then they attached it to the top of the half wall to make sure I couldn't hop over it. Mama said they wanted to keep me safe. As much as I hate that they did all that work because I ran off, I have to admit that it looks good. They even included a friendly looking gnome named Henry who is standing on his hands. (I've been tempted to test the wall because I have a pretty impressive vertical jump, but I thought better of it. I don't want to give them any reason not to trust me.) Building that planter was really unnecessary though, because I now understand that they won't abandon me. I wouldn't hop that wall again for love or money.

Incidents on the interstate

Mama's family lives out of state. After I had been living with her and The Backup for about three weeks, she decided that she wanted to go visit them. Of course she wanted me to go along so she wouldn't be separated from her new bundle of love, and also so she could show me off. This trip required a four hour drive.

Remember, I didn't do very well trying to hitch a ride to Nashville. I had to give that idea up, <u>and</u> I wound up in jail. It wasn't my best day, even though it finally had a happy ending. Had it been my difficulty with cars that got me locked up? I thought surely things would be different this time since I would be in the car with my person. There were no jitters to be had about moving to a new city alone and trying to succeed in a competitive business this time. There was nothing to stress about. This trip was bound to go just fine. I don't want to jump ahead of myself, but it did not work out that way.

Mama and The Backup loaded the car early that morning. Peanut and I happily got into prime napping positions in the back seat. The

Backup settled into the passenger seat while fighting with the radio and his phone, which together he called technology. Mama got into the driver's seat. The three of us, The Backup excluded, since he was busy muttering under his breath and poking buttons on the radio, looked at each other and smiled. Mama and I had on our extra pretty smiles, and Peanut wore her usual short-some-teeth mindless grin. This would be a good trip. Surely.

Then, Mama started the car. Images of those tires coming so close to my face just a few weeks ago jumped to my mind. Immediately I was on high alert and afraid. I needed some comfort. Peanut was still sprawled out next to me on the seat, caring only about sleeping as comfortably as possible. The Backup was still muttering at the technology, but now he had sweat popping out on his forehead. Mama wasn't paying a lick of attention to me either. She was in travel mode, and intent on getting where she wanted to go. I weighed my options for a few minutes, and decided that The Backup was my best bet. I jumped into his lap, and my nerves calmed some when he gave up on the technology and started to pet me.

I did OK until Mama took us onto the interstate. If you don't know about the interstate, let me explain it to you. It's a bunch of roads where crazy people drive really fast while they zig zag across a yellow line. The sight of those cars going so fast was just too much for my little heart. Suddenly, The Backup might as well have been the cop who picked me off the railroad tracks. This would not work. I skittered into Mama's lap, but she pushed me away while The Backup pulled me back. They said something ridiculous like it wasn't safe for me to do that. Of course it was, that's why I was doing it. In Mama's lap was the <u>only</u> place I was safe. There's just no understanding people.

I tried this four times, and still didn't convince them that I really just needed to change my seat. They would have none of that. The

Backup tried wrapping me up in a blanket and getting me comfy in the back seat again. I hopped back as soon as he turned away. Then he tried putting a jacket on and zipping me up in the jacket with him. No go. I squirmed out back into his lap. I will admit that I was 100% totally out of control.

I was desperate. I needed to be close to Mama, but they wouldn't let me in her lap. I had to get close another way, and if I could be in a small space that would help, too. Small places help me feel safe. I was rattled, so it was hard for me to think, but eventually I found my solution. There were some pedals down on the floor at Mama's feet, and behind that, under her chair, was just an open hole. Hey, I could fit in there. It wasn't what I really needed, but it was the best I could do.

I waited for The Backup's grip on me to loosen. When it did, I dove straight for Mama's feet, and squirmed into that hole under her chair as fast as I could. I had made it. My heart finally started to slow to a normal thump rate, but immediately chaos descended. Mama screamed. The Backup screamed. I couldn't see Peanut, but she probably didn't do anything anyway. I saw two big sets of fingers trying to curl under the seat to grab me. Then I felt the car stop moving.

The Backup grabbed me and handed me to Mama. He wasn't especially gentle, either. Now I could see that we had pulled over to the side of the road, and cars were whizzing past us. I thought I might throw up then, but then I realized where I was. In Mama's lap. I had won.

But I hadn't. The Backup started pulling things out of the trunk and stuffing them under the chairs. He slammed the door as he sat back down in his chair, then he took me back from Mama. Oh no, not again. My stomach melted. The throwing up would happen any second now.

We took off again, and I begged myself to calm down. I lifted my head and looked for help from above. It was no use. I had no power against this fear that dug into every inch of me.

I again made some half witted calculations and waited for my moment to strike. The Backup turned his head to look out the window, and I sprung out of his hands like a frog off a diving board. But this time, I went behind Mama's chair. I was hoping The Backup had only stuffed things in the front, and I was rewarded with a wide open path under the chair.

Again I squirmed in, again the screaming, again the pulling over. When the car stopped this time, I knew things were about to get real serious real fast.

When I heard The Backup's car door slam shut, I actually thought about making an escape and walking home. No, that was crazy. Then I would be alone and close to a bunch of cars. And then what would I do at home by myself for days? Nope, my only choice was to just give in and hope for some mercy.

I was grabbed again and handed to Mama. More things were stuffed under both chairs from both sides. I couldn't have gotten in there if I had magically turned myself into gravy.

I think The Backup could see that now I was whipped. His frown got a little smaller and he offered to drive so Mama could hold me. When they swapped chairs, my tightened muscles relaxed. The rest of the trip was a dream.

We had a good time on our visit. I was the star of the show, you know, getting lots of pets and complements. *Oh, how precious. I love how her tail curls up and over her back. Would you look at those cute little ears? One of them flops over just a little. Those snaggle teeth are just darling.* If I had had pudgy cheeks, I believe they would have been pinched off.

Running around in another yard with different flowers to check out was great too. And it seems that when we go on visits, Mama doesn't go to work. Bonus. There was even a creek that reminded me of where I grew up. They called the place where we went Kentucky, but I think that must be another name for heaven.

The night before we were going to go home, I heard The Backup say that he wasn't going with us. He was going to see a friend, and would join us at home in a couple of days. My hackles were up in a flash. How was this going to work? Was Peanut going to drive? There was no way she was smart enough to pass a drivers test. I was too scared to try driving myself. Besides, we were in Mama's car, she would want to drive. The got-to-throw-up feeling was back. I barely slept that night. I was so upset and worried that I couldn't get settled even though I was curled up in the small of Mama's back and under a heavy quilt.

I guess my tired got the best of me, because I woke up in a cage, excuse me, crate, in the back of the car. I would never have agreed to that if I had been awake. How dare she remind me of my time in the klink? I was fit to be tied, but I was in a cage, excuse me, crate, so it didn't really matter.

I started making some noises to let Mama know that I was none too happy. She tried to sweet talk me, some garbage about almost being home, and that it was dangerous for me to get under the seat. Please. I looked over at Peanut, who was *not* in a cage, but splayed on the back seat, sleeping with her tongue hanging out of her mouth. Now instead of being scared, I was mad and only a tiny bit scared.

I kept making noise, but I also started swiping and chewing at the cage bars. I could sense that Mama didn't like this, that it made her nervous. That made me happy, so I just kept it up. I was being careful not to injure myself, but I didn't let Mama know that. OK, that was pretty mean of me, but at the time I felt that it was only fair after what she had done to me.

She was a hot mess by the time we got home, and she promised never to close me in a cage again. I ride in her lap if I want to now. And I always want to.

Puppy love life

Anyone in the public eye gets hounded (nice word choice, huh?) about their love life. It's only a matter of time until my mailbox is overflowing with such questions, so I'm going to address it now. Let me just be upfront about this: I am and will always be a single dog.

I admit that my head is turned by a muscular chested stud like any other girl. Since I'm pretty easy on the eyes myself, I have never had any trouble finding admirers.

During my pupdom, the eligible bachelors, and a few ineligible hopefuls, basically lined the yard waiting to get a look at me. It was pretty embarrassing. I was blushing under my beautiful fur. I have to say that a small part of me did enjoy all the attention, though.

The hard part was being gentle with the boys I wasn't interested in. I didn't want to hurt their feelings, because they obviously had excellent taste in women, but I also had to make it clear that I was in control. It was hard on me to see their sad puppy dog eyes when I turned them down. This happened so many times that I perfected the tactful shake off. I could have spouted off my little speech in my

sleep. My tune had to change when I met my one real love, though.
I was known to flirt with Beau, a dreamy eyed French Bulldog who lived across the creek from me, by getting a little bit closer than necessary. He sure did smell handsome...looked it, too. Oh my, I believe my whiskers are curling just remembering...Anyway, he had the muscular chest I couldn't resist, and an accent to boot. You should have heard him. His bow wows could melt a heart of stone, and he could wrap you around his paw with one woof.

We started our relationship by cricket stomping together. You know what they say about a cricket stomping contest, there's a whole lot of action, but nothing gets done. Everyone knows you can't ever actually stomp on a cricket, but we sure had fun trying (or maybe we were just pretending). Before long, things were starting to get serious. Then we were taking long walks together, sometimes even eating out of the same bowl. One day while we were on a walk, I saw him do a double take looking at a cute little mutt that was chasing her own tail beside the trail we were following.

Well, that made me madder than a wet hen, and something in me snapped. I was reminded of my father, who was led astray by big eyes. I knew if Beau could fall for a dog dumb enough to chase her own tail, I was about to fall into the same trap as my mother. Nope. Not this girl. I would learn from the mistakes of others. I stopped dead in my tracks and watched Beau drool for a few seconds. Before he had even taken his eyes off her, I reared back for just a split second before head butting him and letting fly a few choice words. I ran home as fast as my little legs could go, and made up my mind that from then on, I would be fully devoted to my good-as-real singing career. I didn't shed one tear over that jerk.

I've never looked back. That experience taught me that I don't need some boyfriend, or any dog really, to make me feel special. I am special, and if I don't feel that way, it's my own fault. I really bought into the self affirmation techniques, and pushing my limits in order to improve myself. Working hard on perfecting my singing did wonders for my mindset. I was distracted from my hurting heart, and at the same time I was making progress in something important to me. Setting goals has always been good for my mood.

I really should be thankful for that little mutt beside the trail. If it hadn't been for her, I might still be in Podunkville, scrapping to take care of my own pups all alone. Plus, she wound up dumping Beau too, and in a very humiliating, very public way. OK, OK, since you insist, I'll tell you what happened.

She was at his extended family's monthly picnic, and when he gave her a look she didn't appreciate, she kicked his water bowl so hard that it bruised the side of his muzzle <u>and</u> his ego. You go, girl!

You already know what eventually happened. It turns out that I'm a one person dog, in addition to being a no dog dog (although I have to live with an extra person and another dog). My world revolves around Mama now. I think she hung the moon, and I've never been happier.

Peanut

When I moved into my new house, there was already a dog living there. It was the same one I had met at the jail before I was bailed out. I hadn't paid much attention to her at that time, because I was busy trying to impress Mama so I could earn my freedom. Since I was planning to stay here for good, I figured I better learn to get along with the old girl.

She's a big old mutt, more than twice my size. I know she could fit my whole face in her mouth if she got mad enough. I don't even want to imagine that, because her breath is pretty fierce,
kibble breath plus morning breath. All day long. And it could take the paint off a wall.

Peanut has a temper. I heard a rumor that she used to get mad at Mama's last dog, Maria. It used to make me sad that I'm not Mama's first dog, but she probably needed company way back before she met me. I think this was even before I was born. Anyway, Peanut put a hole in the skin around that dog's neck. That hole didn't do any scary damage, but it did prove that

Peanut can definitely be violent. I've even heard Mama mention that Peanut bit her finger when she was trying to break up a fight between her and Maria. She went after a person who controls her food? That's just crazy.

On the plus side, Peanut is also dumb. I use this to my advantage a lot. If she's got the best relaxing spot by the widows, I bark, then dumb Peanut goes outside to see what's out there, and I take her spot. I'm no dummy.

She is dumb, but she is also a manipulator. I'm not sure how the two go together, but somehow she manages it. I'll give you a recent example. It's so crazy you might be tempted not to believe me. Cross my heart, it's true.

In our basement, there is a big room with a TV and two recliners next to each other across from it. We often sit there in the almost dark to watch TV, and it's just like going to the movies. At least that's what I've heard. I've never been to the movies. Anyway, one of our doggy doors is close by, which is convenient for quick potty breaks during boring movie scenes.

On a Sunday afternoon, Mama and I had just nestled ourselves into one of the recliners to watch a movie. Less than three minutes into the movie, Peanut, who always makes at least two test attempts at the doggy door before coming inside, flies in from the yard without warning. She immediately hops into the empty recliner beside us. Mama and I both notice that Peanut is buzzing. I'm not sure if you are aware of this, but it is unusual for a dog to buzz. We settle back in, just assuming that Peanut is being goofy again, and immediately she hops into our recliner. Peanut's buzzing got louder. I watched Mama's eyes get big as she looked over at Peanut and noticed a bee sitting on her neck. Mama screams, throws me, Peanut, and the blanket we had been wrapped in onto the floor, and hops over to the lightswitch to turn the lights on. Well, sometime during the screaming, throwing, and hopping, the bee had fallen off of

Peanut's neck and was laying on the floor kind of twitching and buzzing. Mama said something about not knowing if it could sting or not, and then she smashed it with her sandal a couple of times. After that, she ran upstairs for the fly swatter which she then used to pick the bee up and throw it outside.

A bee on the neck. I refer to it as Buzzgate. Does Peanut really expect us to think the bee was flying over her and got a wing cramp that forced an emergency landing onto her neck? Honestly, that dog will stop at nothing to disrupt my time with Mama. Like I said, a manipulator.

Peanut is also lazy, and I'm not sure if that's because she's old or just has a bad attitude. Every once in a while, she gets jealous and will try to greet Mama as nicely as I do. While I jump really high and smile, she only manages a half jump and a face like she's got gas. It's pretty sad to watch. She spends most of her time sleeping or looking out the window while she's sprawled out on the couch.

She is definitely <u>not</u> lazy when it comes to food. Peanut likes to eat, and she begs with a persistence I can't help but admire just a little. She only begs from The Backup, though, because she knows it's pointless to beg from Mama. She might not be lazy in this begging area, but she still doesn't want to use any energy if she has zero chance of success.

This is how it goes. She starts by sitting close to The Backup while keeping her eyes on his food. Slowly, she will move closer to the food. Obviously this only works if the food is in a position where she can get closer. If not, she will dance on her hind legs. I'm not even kidding about this. Miss Lazy Dog needs a top hat and cane for her food dance. But often, The Backup is in a place where she is able to get close to him, so the dancing isn't necessary. If she moves slowly enough, he won't even notice until she's right next to the food. I've even seen her a couple of times with her mouth open ready to pounce. But The Backup always notices before she snags a snack, and when he does, he will move her away. This is when her attitude changes. She will come back and start pawing at him. Listening to him, you would think this really ticks him off, but he always winds up handing his dish to Peanut to lick clean. He's such a wimp, but it works out for me. I usually sneak in a lick or two myself.

I learned to guard my food after Peanut stole it a couple of times. Once, Mama noticed and took some food out of Peanut's bowl and gave it to me, but she only caught the kibblenapper once. So now there is no break between appetizer and kibble for me, it's too dangerous. Peanut can suck down my little bowl of food like it's nothing. Like I said, she's not lazy when it comes to food. She is a food thief and warrior.

One day I watched Peanut fight a cat. Well, it really wasn't much of a fight. From my pillow by the window, I saw her sniffing around the bushes in the yard. She loves those bushes, because for some reason our neighbor's shaggy cat uses them for his own special bathroom. I prefer to smell flowers, but to each his own. Suddenly Peanut looked up, and spotted shaggy cat walking into the yard. She got an instant mohawk as the fur all down her spine stood up. She let out her best howl and took off after shaggy cat to scare him away. The only problem was that shaggy cat wasn't scared. He barely even looked at Peanut until they were inches apart. Then he took a couple of steps forward and swiped Peanut across the muzzle. She yelped, tucked tail, and ran straight to the doggy door. I don't think she would have moved any faster if there had been a pile of ham waiting inside for her. That was the first and only time I've felt sorry for Peanut. I would have felt sorry for any dog after what I had just seen. When she came in with that bloody scratch on her muzzle, I scooted over on the pillow so she could rest next to me.

Other dogs

Dogs aren't really my thing. That sounds terrible, and I realize that technically I'm a dog myself, but I have the spirit of a human. Not just any human: a loyal, beautiful, genius human.

I put up with Peanut because I have to. She's old and has been part of the household since way before I was born, so I have to respect that.

Don't think that means that she's the alpha. That is definitely not the case. I can be extremely submissive with my people, but not with other dogs. Peanut is The Backup's dog anyway, so I get Mama all to myself. It works out pretty well, I think, keeping us kind of separated. We spend a lot of time in our own little worlds, much more with our people than each other. And, I do get some education on what not to do by watching her, so there is some benefit to having her around. Age does not always bring wisdom. I'll leave it at that.

We get along pretty well, since I've only had to growl at her a couple of times when she went after something that was mine. We all have to make small sacrifices for the pack, and getting along with Peanut is my sacrifice.

It's not that I hate other dogs. I just don't think I have much in common with your average Rover. I have great respect for my mother, being a single parent and all. I also love all my siblings, but especially Aarfah. I have to believe that somewhere in this big world there is at least a sprinkling of other strong, sophisticated dogs like us, but I haven't met one yet.

The closest I've come to having a real friend besides Aarfah was little Biscuit. Biscuit was a Pekingese that lived next door to us in Podunkville. Her house had the TV that my mother and I would watch through the window sometimes.

Biscuit was like a real live fairy tale with gorgeous hair. I've heard that her breed came from emperor's palaces in China, and I believe it. She had a round black face that looked like a teddy bear. I don't know how she breathed through that flat nose, but she sure was beautiful. She was about my size, but most of that size was long silky hair. I would have felt very dumpy and ugly compared to her if I hadn't been so impressed with her.

We watched the news together every night. I would get there early, and take my spot on the plant stand that was on the patio just outside her window. She would walk into the room just as the theme music started playing, and would wink at me before sitting on a fluffy cushion right in front of the TV. She never told her people that I was out there. She could have, but I guess she didn't want them to run me off. Maybe she was lonely. I think the wink meant that our news watching was our secret. We sat quietly in our places until the program ended. Then we both stood, nodded to each other, and walked away. Sometimes words aren't necessary between friends.

A couple of times, I've been forced to go to the dog park. The other dogs were happily barking and wrestling with each other. Not me.

I spent my time with Mama, either sitting on a bench or sniffing the park's history while walking around the perimeter of the fence. She was trying to get me interested in the other small dogs, but I shut that down pretty quick. I don't want to share toys or play chase. The toys are covered with slobber, and playing chase is too much like exercise. Not to mention that most dogs just aren't up to my standard. They can be so uncivilized, like they were never domesticated. I've seen them roll in mud, eat things off the ground, unspeakable things really. So the dog park hasn't been tried in a long time, and I don't think Mama will make the mistake of socializing me again any time soon.

I do enjoy going on walks, although I try to make it seem that I don't by not helping get into my harness. Enthusiasm can be so tacky. The human equivalent of not helping with the harness is being fashionably late. I'm that girl.

Our walks are usually around the neighborhood, but sometimes we go to a park instead. Peanut walks on one side of Mama, and I walk on the other side. Every once in a while, Peanut doesn't come when the leashes are pulled out of the big basket where our things are kept. That's a great day because I get a walk with just Mama, and I don't have to try to wait patiently while Peanut smells <u>every blade of grass</u>.

If we happen to meet another dog on a walk, I stop and let Peanut do her silly socializing, but I don't acknowledge the new dog. I stand beside Mama and look straight ahead the whole time because as you know, I value my reputation. I can't be seen hanging out with just anyone. A few times, the dog we meet will step right up to me and insist on sniffing me. It's always been a boy. They just don't respect boundaries, and let's face it, I'm pretty irresistible. So then I growl from deep down in my throat to make my opinion clear. It's not that I'm better than them, we're just not the same. You get it, right?

Bladder issues

Since moving into my current and forever home, there have always been two doggy doors available to me. I love this feature, because I can come and go as I please, and maybe just as importantly, I don't have to notify someone every time I need to potty. Nobody needs to know <u>all </u>my business. I like that my people respect my ability to take care of myself.

That said, it is very important that Mama <u>never</u> potty alone. I choose a nice safe place to go, out in the yard on solid ground. Mama, for whatever reason, insists on sitting on a cold hard chair in a little room. And I think there's water under a hole in the chair. This has to be uncomfortable and is for sure dangerous, but I guess she doesn't realize it. So I have to watch out for her, because no one loves her like I do.

Because of this fantastic doggy door situation at home, someone in the rumor mill is bound to say that I'm not housebroken. Just because Peanut might or might not be doesn't mean that I have a problem. Let me assure you that nothing about me is broken, and I also do know how to do my business outside. In fact, if the weather is bad, I can hold it for quite some time. It's better to not muddy my paws or get wet fur if it's not totally necessary. Only a real emergency is worth ruining a good fur day.

There is a serious issue that affects me called piddling. Not the kind where you just waste time doing little silly stuff. In this case, what piddling means is that when someone (usually Mama or The Backup) approaches me to pet me, especially if they just got home, I am so happy that my heart gets excited too. It grows a good bit and winds up pushing against my bladder. The result is that a drop or two of you know what might escape if I haven't just recently been in the yard.

According to doggy tradition, the root cause of piddling is a genetic predisposition to hyper love. It's an extra gene that only a select few have. I'm going to be brave enough to say that the huge love capacity I was born with makes me a better dog. While piddling is a serious disease, and sometimes those who have it are punished for it, it doesn't do any damage to me. My heart goes right back to normal size after a few seconds. It doesn't mess with my energy level or change my water drinking needs. My life expectancy is not shortened at all. So basically, there is one disease that is actually good for you, and I have it.

Since I'm a talented actress as well as a singer, I can also make myself potty if the situation requires it. You see, not a single person I have ever met realizes that piddling is because of hyper love. They usually think it means that I'm scared, or trying to get revenge. I think you can understand how I might have fun with this.

If The Backup is mad at me for cleaning his ear too much and tells me to leave him alone, I can act scared. These eyes of mine can get huge, and I can scrunch my neck and shoulders back, even shiver a little bit. I'm truly convincing, I tell you. The real trick is that while I'm doing all this, I'm thinking about Mama. Thinking of her makes my heart grow and push on my bladder. The result is that I piddle, and all of a sudden The Backup feels sorry for me because he thinks I'm scared of what he might do to me. I get out of trouble a lot that way. Sometimes I am amazed by my talents.

Let's just say it's also theo... What is it, Mama? Theoretically possible that I could act my way into piddling as part of a plan to take center stage for myself when Peanut is getting the attention. Not jealousy, no, not me. A little payback maybe. Just try to steal Mama from me again. Eat my kibble, see what happens. Try to borrow my sweater. I double dog dare you.

Fashion

Dogs and humans everywhere without a doubt want to know my take on fashion. I think it's a highly individual choice, and that your fashion choices should reflect your personality or dogonality, whichever applies. Fashion is for you, not to impress others. It's also all about confidence. If you feel happy and comfortable in something, you are doing fashion right, whether anyone else likes it or not.

I prefer to spend the vast majority of my time naked as a jaybird. As a dog with a short coat, I never need to hide a bad haircut or worry about bad fur days. If you got it, flaunt it, I say. But that's just me. Remember what I said about confidence? I've got a good bit of it, and with good reason.

Another thing that comes with my short coat is that I can get cold easily. So when it's very cold outside, or if there's snow on the ground, I will allow Mama to dress me for comfort's sake. To be honest, I look forward to it since it doesn't happen very often. If I dressed up every day, it wouldn't feel like a special moment.

I have a ski jacket that would make most dogs drool with envy. It is kind of an ombré, with bands running around me that get darker toward my tail. It zips up the back and has a bit of a mock turtleneck. There are even metal rings on the back to attach my leash so there aren't any weird looking harness bumps along my back. I usually wear it as intended, but sometimes I feel saucy and insist that Mama leave the mock turtleneck portion unzipped. I'm short, so I like that the jacket protects my belly from cold snow and grass. And let's just put it out there: It's not all about warmth, I work that ski jacket. I get so many admiring looks and compliments from dogs and humans when I wear it that it's almost scandalous.

I really enjoy Christmas with all the shiny decorations, and of course there are extra snacks waiting to be had. I was given several Christmas sweaters to help me celebrate, but there is only one that I like. Let me tell you, it's an exquisite piece of art. First off, it's black, which is always classy. There is a red edge around the bottom which sits just above my tail when I wear it. There is red at the top too, in the form of a turtleneck. I guess I just like wearing a turtleneck to help draw attention to my face. The main piece of decoration is a 3D snowman. The snowman himself is a silky white fabric, and he's wearing a polka dotted scarf with <u>real fringe</u> that hangs free. A red top hat sits on his head at a jaunty angle. Snowflakes and peppermint bones surround him. Peppermint bones! Talk about mind blowing happiness on a sweater!

At this time, the snow jacket and Christmas sweater is the extent of my wardrobe because I am very choosy. If at some time a piece of clothing grabs my interest with its amazingness, I will wear it without giving any thought to what any person or any dog might think about it. I just haven't run across anything lately that doesn't detract from my natural good looks. I do have an extra special hat that I have only worn once, but we'll talk more about that later.

As for paw-wear, you already know my thoughts about boots. In general, I feel like I can't prance quite as well if I'm wearing any type of shoes, so I choose to skip them. You do you. Some dogs can make shoes look great. Since I don't wear shoes or even socks, my nails are always on display. I don't paint them, but I am meticulous in making sure that they are well trimmed. I spend lots of time on them, actually.

I never got into the goth or emo scenes, but I had a short futuristic phase some time ago. This was back when I was still dreaming of

going on tour. I could just see myself rocking it in a puffy shimmery skirt, tons of bangle bracelets, and a spiky headband. It still would be a cool look, but it seems like a great choice for the stage, not my comfy home.
Besides, my style has changed since then. I'm more of a classic starlet type now, I think. Maybe there's an A-line dress and a string of pearls in my future.

I know there are a few pictures floating around of me wearing a multicolored striped sweater. I never liked that sweater, but the pictures were taken while I was getting used to my new home and people.

I was still in the phase where I was really trying extra hard to make sure Mama and The Backup loved me. It was kind of a sad transitional time when I didn't have enough self-esteem, honestly. All I can say is that jail really does a number on your spirit.

Thankfully, things are better now. I did attend a few informal therapy sessions with a miniature Poodle who lives around the corner. She helped me to achieve my current better state where I can now assert (she taught me that word) my wants without feeling guilty. Her stance on individuality and elegance is amazing. If anyone is interested in her services, get in touch, and I'll set up a referral. I just don't want to publish her name and info because she values her privacy as much as I do.

Back to the original topic. I reserve dressing up for certain specific occasions. This is just how I choose to do things. If you want to wear ruffles and a bow tie every day, go for it! Pleather and feathers on Fridays? Why not? For me, though, spending the majority of my time clothesless means that I have to pay extra special attention to hygiene.

Hygiene

I am a bit of a perfectionist when it comes to hygiene. Hygiene, by the way, is a fifty cent word that means staying clean and neat. I just can't go along with the sloppy habits of my generation. I think it reflects badly on a dog when things aren't quite up to snuff.

I've mentioned the amount of effort I put into my nails. I like to keep them short so I don't click when I walk. It's just tacky, begging for attention like that. I don't feel the need to announce myself, but believe me, I will still make an entrance everywhere I go. I also file my nails into perfectly even points because I think it's pretty, and elongating (is that the right word?) for my legs. I'm practical, too. I realize that with my looks comes the burden of frequent jealousy and the possibility that I might have to defend myself. I'm a pacifist at heart. That's why I'm writing this book, to cut off any problems before they start. That said, if I'm attacked, I will come off the chain with no intentions of backing down.

I also like to keep my feet very clean. I go lots of places on my feet, and I don't want to carry dirt all over creation with me, especially not near my bed or food. So when I come inside, I will clean myself up at a mat. First I put my front paws down and stretch backwards, wiping them as I go. Then I'll set all four paws on the mat and kick with my back legs almost like I'm doing roundhouse kicks. This gets any nasties off before I can spread them around. On top of that, I will lick my paws several times a day. I'm a short-haired dog, but I've noticed that the fur on my paws can get a little unruly after a few zoomies or rolls in the yard. Licking the fur makes it lay down very neatly, and I've noticed over time that I've developed a faint pink tinge to my toes. It's really subtle and pretty. I'm not sure if the licking does it, but if it ain't broke...

I have a highly controversial method for cleaning my face. Don't be disappointed in me until you hear me out. I use the cat method. Terrible, I know, but it works really well. Let me share how this works in case you're unfamiliar. Basically, I use the sides of my paws like washcloths. I lick my paws and rub them down my face. It's disgusting when cats do it, but dang if they don't have clean faces. In addition to smoothing my fur, the cat method keeps my face spotless and soft. It even gets the overnight eye boogers out. Every once in a while, Mama will have to get a stubborn one for me, but the cat method works great in general. Shoot. Maybe I shouldn't have said that, because now you know I get eye boogers. Oh well, honesty can be painful sometimes.

Unlike most dogs, I have no problem with getting my teeth brushed. I never argue when Mama gets the toothbrush out. I understand the importance of good oral care because I've seen the commercials. I want to keep my chompers looking healthy and perfect, unlike dumb Peanut who had to have three teeth pulled. Now she just looks goofy when she smiles. She probably had a goofy smile before her teeth were pulled, but I'm a good girl, so I'll give her the benefit of the doubt. My vet said I have the teeth of a much younger dog. Not that I'm old, I'm just in good shape.

I like to have my teeth brushed, but I've made it clear that I will tolerate only mint toothpaste. Good breath is important, and mint is good medicine for halitosis. This is a disease I never want to have. It sounds and smells like a terrible thing. Also, the only real alternative flavor for toothpaste is bacon, and bacon is, besides not good for fresh breath, also fattening. Bacon is made from pigs, and pigs are fat, so if I rub pigs on my teeth I'm going to get fat too, right? When you're my size, well under twelve pounds, you can't afford to gain even an ounce. It would affect my looks, make me run out of breath easily, and maybe even mean that I can't fit into my favorite outfits.

Mama says she's careful with my weight because of my joints. I think that's got to do with the bones in my legs somehow, but all my parts work just fine, so I'm not too worried about my joints. Still, Mama measures out my food every day, and although we don't have the same reasons for watching what I eat, I appreciate her help. I'll admit this: it's hard to stop when there's still kibble in the bowl. Only so much willpower can fit into this cute little body. So measuring is a great solution.

I find sneezes to be both disturbing and unsanitary. In fact, when I hear someone sneeze, I always look to make sure they cover their sneeze and keep things clean. Since I couldn't come up with a way to cover my own sneezes, I learned another way to deal with them. I learned how to keep myself from sneezing. Impressive, I know, but it's not really as hard as it sounds.

Over time, I learned that there are a few things that make me need to sneeze. Grass up to my shoulder, walking around in the yard right after it's been mowed, and for some reason, tulips. So I stay away from those things. I don't walk in tall grass, I stay inside when the lawn mower is out, and I smell azaleas, roses, or buttercups instead of tulips. This works out very well for me, because there are three azalea bushes in the front yard, and five rose bushes in the back yard that I can get to whenever I want. The rose bush in the middle is special. It smells as good as an angel burp. (Did you know that the cut grass can turn your fur green? I've seen Peanut with green legs and a green chest from rolling on the cut grass.)

A conservative estimate is that these changes in my habits reduce sneezing by 74%. No matter how careful I am, there are times when I feel like my sneezer is about to bust. This is, by the way, the worst feeling in the world, like having a bumble bee fly up your nose and start to practice the hula hoop. When I feel that, I rub my tongue against the front top part of the roof of my mouth. This stops the sneeze every time, and I don't end up shooting snot out my nose. That's pretty hygienic, I would say.

I consent to baths without making much trouble. Well, I take showers, actually, like an adult. Mama had a hand held shower installed in the bathroom at just the right height for my showers. She uses special shampoo made with oatmeal to keep my skin from getting dry and itchy. She's so thoughtful. However, I refuse to allow the hair dryer anywhere near me. I will allow a little drying with a fluffy towel, and then I head to a warm spot. I learned a long time ago that although I have straight short hair, I can still get a little frizzy unless I air dry.

So I get a little help to stay at the top of my game. Mostly, though, I'm a self cleaning, self maintaining dog. That's the way I like it.

Graduating from the groomer

One beautiful warm day, I walked with Mama and Peanut to the groomer. It was just down the street and around the corner. We try to be eco-conscious, you know. Don't use gas unless you really need to, that sort of thing.

Anyway, walks give me a chance to see and be seen, so I'm always happy to go unless it's raining or very cold outside. Even when it's very cold, I like to take short walks in my beautiful clothes. On our walks, I also get a chance to see if there are any new yard features in the neighborhood that I should request for home, like the good looking outdoor water dish I saw last month. I can't help but love it when the neighborhood dogs bark as I walk past. I might take a quick look at the loudmouth, but usually, I keep walking like nothing is happening. I never bark back. I don't want to seem too desperate for friends.

The bad part about this particular trip was the destination. I hadn't realized what a groomer was when we started on our journey. It wasn't until we got there that my nose told me what that place was. Even if I had known what a groomer was ahead of time, I probably would have still gone just for the nice walk and to give moral support. Sticking with the pack, you know. If I had realized the true purpose of the visit to the groomer, I would have refused to go.

When we started crossing the parking lot to the shop, I started to have a sinking suspicious feeling about the terrible things that happened inside. I'm not opposed to looking my best, actually, I'm all for it. I just choose to take on that responsibility myself, unlike Peanut who really doesn't care about anything except getting lots and lots of food. What can I say? It's just the truth. When we went in, there was no more doubt about the place, but there was hope because I waited in the lobby with Mama while Peanut had her peticure. Boy, I was glad it wasn't me. Everything was fine. It was a pretty place, covered in pictures of happy looking dogs, and it smelled like lavender perfume. Then came the surprise: I was expected to have a peticure too.

The injustice of it all still raises my hackles. I do an exceptionally perfect job taking care of my nails, so I have no idea why anyone would think I need help in that area. Hoping against hope that I was just going for a nice brushing, I allowed myself to be carried off by a lady who should not be doing nails other than her own. Her nails were as ugly as homemade sin. She started up that horribly loud grinder, and I gritted my pearly whites in an effort to restrain myself. I would give this a chance for Mama's sake, even if it did hurt my pride and eardrums. When that grinder touched my delicate beautiful nail, I almost came unglued. I let her finish that one, but when she loosened her grip on my paw to reposition for the next nail, I couldn't handle it anymore. I could have taken a chunk out of her right then, but instead I let out a short courtesy growl. When she didn't move the grinder away from me, I let loose and bit her.

Before you jump to conclusions, know that I hadn't totally snapped. It wasn't a real bite. I could have drawn blood if I had wanted to. I didn't even break the top layer of skin. All I really did was nip to tell her to back off. Maybe I learned a little something from Wurfy after all, although I think I showed more restraint than she would have in the situation. I pride myself on not being impulsive.

Well, that nip was enough for the lady with ugly nails to get the picture. She immediately turned off the grinder, put it down, and carried me back out to Mama. She didn't yell at me or hurt me, but in my opinion, she was a bit more flustered than she really needed to be. To her credit, when she told Mama about what happened, she said that I hadn't injured her at all. I think I embarrassed Mama a little, because we walked home pretty fast and didn't get to stop and smell the grass by my favorite dogwood tree. I kind of felt like I was in time out. Anyway, Mama said that we weren't going back there because I'm not allowed in the groomer's place anymore. That is just fine with me because I have a natural sort of low maintenance beauty.

My super singing

You might remember that this whole adventure of a new life started when I took a risk and went out into the world to pursue a singing career. That didn't go quite according to plan. I'm in a different place now, equally good if not better than what I had hoped for. Here's the turning point: since I've found my person, I don't feel the need for a national or global stage anymore. I won't lie, the money would be nice. I could buy a lot of bling with millions of dollars. Going on tour and missing out on time with Mama would be terrible, though. Even staying home, though, music hasn't left me. The fact is that I still love to sing. And I like to have an audience.

Anytime we have a visitor in the house, I sing one of my specially composed songs. Of course, I don't start to sing until I've thoroughly checked the visitor out from behind Mama's legs. My guess is that more than nine out of ten times this method, which includes a special air sniff and visual once over, does the job. The other few times it's a little more dangerous, and requires that I approach the visitor, stare at them briefly while cocking my head (looking for signs of nervousness), and take a small lick on their right big toe. That's where the human goodness meter is located.

This procedure is one thing I learned in jail by watching another inmate that has been very helpful in real life. Jack might have acted immature most of the time, but he was smart. I'll give him that.

People might think that my spot behind Mama proves that I'm a scaredy dog, but I can assure you that I have to stay close to her in case she needs protection. Keeping her safe is really all left up to me. Lazy Peanut wouldn't lift a paw if there was trouble, except maybe to ask for a treat. The Backup would try, but because he's human, he just can't sense danger as well or as early as a dog can.

Assuming that protection isn't necessary, I use my singing voice to show off a little while trying to make the visitor feel welcome. A twofer, you might say. They <u>always</u> laugh when I sing. There are two possible reasons for them to laugh. One is that they appreciate my wonderful song, excessive talent, and amazing level of effort. The other is that they think I sound terrible. I can't believe that every visitor to the house would be crazy enough to think my beautiful singing is terrible, so I believe that the first reason must be the true cause of the laughter. They just can't help themselves, and the appreciation bubbles right out of them.

This excellent feedback makes me want to try even harder to please everyone. I forgot to mention that not only the visitors laugh, but Mama and The Backup, too. So now I've started practicing more when it's just the family at home. Peanut appreciates good music, but she won't participate when people are around. Whether she's shy or just smart about this one thing, I don't know. Anyway, when it's just us, Peanut can't help but join in. This is fine with me, because she makes it extra obvious that I have a great voice. She has zero talent. She has that hound dog bellow that's only good for scaring away ugly creatures when you're out in the middle of the woods. I haven't told her that, because it's just not in my nature to be rude, but I sure think it. You know, if you can't say something good... I know everyone in our neighborhood thinks it too.

You might be interested in my singing posture, maybe just out of curiosity, or maybe because you would like some pointers. Either way, I'm happy to share. It is very important that you always stand to sing. I don't know where my diaphragm is or what it looks like, but it seems to do its job better when I stand up, and that means I sound better. I also find that straightening my throat improves the sound. I do this by lifting my head straight up like I'm looking at the ceiling. I think giving my voice a straight shot out of my muzzle keeps it sounding sweet and strong. I have been known, if I'm especially feeling the sound or lyrics, to lift up off my front paws. This is my signature move, although I never planned it that way. It's just my natural reaction to the beauty of song.

I find it best not to sing on a full stomach. Mama and The Backup have agreed not to have anyone over right after meal time. They thought it was a weird request until I explained it to them. What irritates me is that sometimes people just show up uninvited right after I've eaten. I can't be rude, as I just pointed out. I still sing, and I give it my best, but it's just a little shy of perfection.

Many famous and excellent singers have either big mouths or special teeth. You won't have to think long to come up with a list of these folks, I'm talking really famous. Anyway, I'm no exception to this. My mouth is elegantly small and in proportion to the rest of me. What I do have is special teeth. They are pearly white as you would expect and also elegantly small. Here's the special part. Are you ready? They don't all point in the same direction! What this means is that the sound comes out of my mouth and is pushed in different directions, easily filling an entire room. It's like I have a built in megaphone, but the megaphone is kept in a really cute case.

Since we're on the subject, I will add that I can also write lyrics like a true poet. I don't write very often because I really have to feel it in my bones to write. Let me tell you about one of my best songs.

I wrote it after I broke my first heart. His name was Gizmo and I was tempted to like him because, well... he had a nice chest, but he was also super funny. He could crack a joke about anything. One day, though, he went too far and called me a loony goony, and the way he said it... He was holding his tail funny, and I knew he really meant that he thought I was crazy. That didn't sit right. I told him to keep his paws off me. The whole situation hurt my heart, so I wrote this song:

> *I revenge you,*
> *May a tick suck your eyelid off,*
> *You lost the great thing - me,*
> *I am the queenest,*
> *Woof, woof, grr*

Now have a little grace, this was originally written in Dogspeak which is a much more beautiful language than English.

Beach babe

Khaki, how can you live with yourself, taking extravagant vacations while there are so many strays in the world? You should be using your fame and fortune as a platform to help others. Grr. I can almost hear a reporter grilling me, and, to some degree, I've wondered about it myself.

Well, for one thing, my vacations do nothing to hurt strays. It's kind of like kids being told to finish their plates because someone around the world is hungry. Calories can't be transferred from one person to someone else halfway around the world, and by staying home I'm not magically giving a dog a forever home. So it's not a fair question, but if you keep reading, you'll agree that my one real vacation was not extravagant.

Mama and The Backup decided that we were going to take a road trip some time ago, just the four of us. Yes, Peanut had to go too. The Backup loves that mutt for some reason. There was a bit of arguing about what kind of car to take and where to go, but in the end, we drove around the coast of Florida in a minivan.

This was a strange looking vehicle, much bigger than Mama's car. There were two seats in the front, and the rest of it was mattress, like straight off someone's bed, mattress. What a specialized thing to rent. One of my beds was brought along, too, and was placed on top of the mattress right behind and between the seats. I spent most of my time in Mama's lap, but I did sit on my bed a few times while she drove. The Backup did most of the driving, because, well, they had learned something about riding with me.

I got to spend two nights in a hotel. A hotel is kind of like a whole bunch of little apartments stacked up, but with some nice extras. I noticed lots of looks and smiles from everyone, but I was never offered a key to the room or special turndown service with a treat left on the pillow. Peanut and I had to eat our regular kibble out of our regular bowls, so I guess it wasn't a five star hotel. It sure wasn't a five bone hotel.

I can doggy paddle like a pro, but since it was a little cool out (it was January), I decided against getting in the hotel's outdoor pool. I'm more of a hot tub kind of girl, anyway. Forget all that swimming exercise when I can be toasty and relax at the same time. I was just about to test the water with my paw when someone turned on the bubbles. It was so loud I almost jumped out of my fur. I didn't think I could handle being down <u>in</u> all that racket. So instead of getting in, I backed up a couple of steps, and snugged into a towel so I could keep warm and muffle the sounds of the bubbles. I was content to watch Mama and The Backup kick back in the hot tub, especially when she pointed out how cute I looked with the towel over my head. Peanut was sprawled out like a slug, keeping her eyes open just enough to watch an ant walk across the patio. She doesn't know how to appreciate the finer things in life. I might have mentioned that before.

There were no dog beds in the hotel room, but we all sleep together anyway, like a real pack, so that was ok with me. I have heard that some people make their dogs sleep in cages, excuse me, crates, and I just can't understand that. Sorry, I got a little sidetracked. I was talking about the hotel. I already complained about the total lack of snacks. The only real problem with the hotel was that I never found even one doggy door. Mama took us out pretty often for sniffs and potty breaks, though. Hey, now that I think of it, maybe I should have Mama leave a review. That hotel could really improve if I gave them some suggestions. Everyone is entitled to my opinion, you know.

We drove a lot, so meals needed to be quick. It seems that Florida is a big place, and we had a lot of driving to do. A couple of times Mama went to a grocery store and got sandwiches for herself and The Backup. Mostly, though, they preferred to eat at restaurants.

The injustice of the restaurant situation really ruffled my fur. Canine discrimination is real, folks. Peanut and I were only allowed on the patios of two restaurants while we were on this trip, we couldn't even set paw inside. There were no bowls of water, nothing for us. Dogs have bellies, too, so we should be able to go inside and eat as long as we pay. What a terrible way to treat potential customers. Mama and The Backup understand this. Most of the time The Backup would get something from inside the restaurant and bring it out. Then we all had a picnic together on the mattress in the back of the minivan. It wasn't glamorous, but at least they took a stand by staying with us.

I had never seen the ocean before. You would think someone with my level of class would be well traveled, but sadly this hasn't been the case. I've been to Kentucky (heaven) to visit family, downtown, a few stores, a few parks, that's it. I could count on one paw the parks I've been to, because we go to the same parks over and over again. I had no idea what to expect when Mama said we were going to the beach. The beach, I found out, is the outline of the ocean.

I couldn't believe my eyes at first. The ocean goes on forever, I guess, and when I got close, I could see that it moves. We went to a special dog beach, but Peanut was the only other dog there. The silly thing would get way out there towards the water and then run back when the water turned around and started getting close to her. I saw what was happening and just stayed past where the water went. The ground along the water was covered in a special kind of dirt called sand. It comes in big round pieces that like to stick to everything. Sandy paws are one thing, but wet sandy paws would have been terrible to get clean. It's just best to avoid some messes.

The ocean makes noise kind of like the hot tub, but much softer and I think it could make you fall asleep. If I had had a blanket, I would have been snoozing in no time. Instead, we walked by the water and searched for what I think are called shells... yep, Mama said they were shells. The beach looked like a mess with garbage all over it, but up close, the garbage is just shells, which turned out to be the used houses of little water creatures. Most of them had pretty lines and swirls on them.

I'll be better prepared the next time I go to the beach. I checked; fur counts as a bathing suit, so I don't have to get dressed unless I feel like it. I will have some cute round sunglasses made for myself, and I'll make sure to take a blanket to stretch out on, and an umbrella to help keep me cool. A collapsible bowl for doggy sports drinks would come in handy too. I have no intention of getting in the water and messing up my fur, but I feel sure someone will invite me to play volleyball. Oh, and a magazine with lots of pictures, and a box of pupsicles.

Play

You might hear from those wanting to make me look bad that I play childish games. Well, that used to be the case, I was just a young pup once, you know, but not anymore. When I first moved in, there were two games I played with Mama so I could get in my time with her. I now understand that I don't have to play the games so we can spend time together, and since I'm more mature now, that suits me just fine.

The games I played really are great games, but I've outgrown them now. I still have plenty of happy memories. The first game was Sock, and the second was Scratch.

Mama noticed that I sometimes liked to bring her things she needed, like a washcloth or piece of paper, so she got creative. She started tying knots in socks and throwing them around the house for me to grab and bring back to her. At first, she tried to just throw regular socks, but putting knots in them makes them fly better. So she couldn't put the sock on, but it was still fun even though the sock wasn't useful anymore. It's kind of like Fetch, but using a knotted up sock is way more classy than a dirty old stick.

She would try to trick me by acting like she threw when she didn't, but I almost never fell for it. I also noticed that I could slide when I ran on the wooden floor, so sometimes I would run a little harder than I needed to just to see how far I could slide without bumping into something. The hall between the bathroom and coat closet was the best sliding spot. I would even dance with the sock a little before giving it back. We laughed a lot. Even The Backup laughed, and he can be grumpy sometimes.

What does a Khaki laugh sound like? I thought you might be

wondering. It's almost identical to panting. In fact most people never notice anything different happening, but you can tell if you watch closely because I will also be smiling. Most dogs laugh like this, but we have our share of snorters, too. Pugs mostly.

We spent a lot of quality time playing Sock back in the day. Mama thought I was such a smart girl for bringing the sock right back to her, which is of course true. It was the whole point of the game. Peanut is so lazy that when The Backup tries to play fetch with her, she just looks at him. Since I know Dogspeak, I know she's asking him why he just threw away something he wanted. She spares all effort.

Although I've stopped playing Sock like a puppy, I will still on occasion use a sock to express myself. To give you an example, our neighbor dog Buster came to our house for a week-long vacation a while back. One day when Mama was in the kitchen with him, actually giving him belly rubs if you can believe it, I got seriously upset. That dog was nothing but an attention hog. I found one of my old knotted socks in the corner of the bedroom, and without thinking, I grabbed it in my mouth. Then I strutted right over to her, and while she watched, I flung it down on the floor as hard as I could. She never apologized, but let me tell you, a point was made, and she didn't touch that belly again when I was around.

The second game, Scratch, was another of Mama's inventions. Between the time I was kicked out of the groomer's and when she realized that I trim and maintain my own nails, she created Scratch as a way to keep my nails in good shape. She got a big piece of wood and covered it with sandpaper. Then she filled a little bowl with kibble, and we would go out onto the deck. She sat down, and placed the wood down in front of her. She would have me put my front paws on the sandpaper, and then she threw a piece of kibble just behind me and to one side. When I turned to go for the kibble, I was filing my nails!

It seems that I'm not the only smart one in the family.

We spent a lot of time playing Scratch, because this method of nail filing was not only fun but also pretty slow. Neither one of us got tired of playing, though. The game didn't make us use a whole lot of energy, and what I used, I got back right away in food.

I will admit that I was especially drawn to Scratch not only for the Mama time, but also for the extra kibble I got when we played. One annoying problem with the game was that it was pretty much impossible to keep the food guzzling Peanut away while we played. Quite a few games ended early for that reason, and I wouldn't talk to Peanut for the rest of the day because she ruined my fun. When Mama realized I took care of my nails independently, she decided that Scratch wasn't worth the hassle of fighting Peanut. We had a good run, though.

The games I play now are more intellectual. That's another fifty cent word. Mind games, you might say. Like training The Backup that 3:00 is time for second food. We're getting there, but I still have to figure out how to get him to look at the clock more often. My favorite mind game is convincing Peanut that there's a giant piece of invisible cheese at the bottom of the water bowl. She falls for it every time, and I love watching her shove her whole big face in the bowl. The water dripping off her ears makes me crack up, but she also gets an eye booger cleaning that way, so I guess it's a win win.

Don't let anyone tell you that I play with a monkey. I <u>used</u> to play with a monkey. There was a really nice lady named Glenna who lived across the street from Mama. She gave me a stuffed monkey, and that's what made it special, not that it was a toy. I liked Glenna because even though she didn't have a dog, she loved all little dogs. She would talk to me and pat me softly on my apple head every chance she got. She was one of the good people, and it was sad when she moved away.

Playing with that monkey was kind of like spending time with my friend. It had long floppy arms and legs that flew all over the place when I shook it. It also had a noise box, and it screamed when I bit it just right. I say had because I finally tore that monkey up after playing with it too hard for a few weeks. Now, don't spread this around, but something inside me liked to hear that monkey scream. It made me feel tough, like I had some power.

Delivery drivers

I'm choosy about which humans I like. There are strict standards they have to meet...no cat smell, knee caps low enough that I can take them out if I have to, you know, the normal stuff. Making this decision to approve of someone or not requires close contact. Usually, even more than when I'm deciding if it's safe to let someone be around Mama. Just because someone isn't dangerous doesn't mean they're one of the good people. The process of making a decision gets extra difficult when the person stays separated from me by a window or yard, meaning they don't come inside to me and I don't get outside to them.

I've had to learn to rely on instinct, experience, and limited assessment in a lot of cases. Maybe it's a little less important to assess someone who doesn't actually get in the house or close to me and my pack family. Well, so far there haven't been any disasters, knock on wood.

I'm used to the mailman. He does his job every day and leaves like a good person should. I know he isn't going to cause any trouble, so I don't make a big deal about his arrival. If I feel like it, I'll bark one small woof of acknowledgement, if not, I don't say anything. I only have two problems with the mailman, but that really isn't so bad. First, he doesn't always come at the same time every day, and second, he never asks my permission when he sends someone else to do his job. Oh well, humans are rarely perfect.

Sometimes people walk down the street with a dog or pushing a stroller. Unless they look especially menacing, like they're dressed in ninja gear, or are letting their dog sniff in my front yard, I just ignore them. I've heard Mama say that you should never trust a man wearing a pinky ring, but I get confused about which finger is a pinky, so I don't really know what to look for. Wait, she says it's the short finger. I'll probably forget again in a minute. If anyone has a suggestion for a catchy way to remember where a pinky is on the hand, send it to me, and I would be super thankful.

The special and important people, though, are delivery drivers. These are the ones I wait and hope for. Whole days and even weeks can go by without me seeing one, and that is disappointing. Delivery drivers are my favorite, because they are exciting and unpredictable. I get annoyed with the mailman because even though I know he's coming every day, he doesn't have a schedule. Not knowing if a delivery driver is coming at all is the exciting part. Their visits are always a surprise, and I love surprises!

Sometimes these people park big trucks outside the house, sometimes it's a van down the road a little bit. They might be wearing shorts and a baseball hat, or maybe jeans and a polo shirt. Then the person comes and leaves things, usually boxes but sometimes huge fat pouches, on the porch or carport. The real mystery is what's in the usually boxes but sometimes pouches. It's kind of like Christmas. I definitely prefer these trucks to the loud truck that comes every week and flips the trash can. I think it's too loud, and besides it takes away that great smelling trash instead of leaving presents behind.

Whenever one of these giving trucks arrives, I bark once, just to let Mama and The Backup know about it. Then I wag my tail and try to look extra cute. When the package is brought in the house, sometimes it has a bag of yummy bones for me! Usually it's something boring for The Backup, but I think the driver leaves a present for me if I pose just right. This is one of my powers.

My magic pose doesn't work on one driver. He has an Adam's apple bigger than my head. He wears a polo shirt, but unlike everyone else who does, he also wears a huge chain around his neck. I could forgive a big Adam's apple and bad taste in jewelry, but this guy <u>never</u> brings me anything. When I see him get out of his truck, I actually frown at him and turn my back to the window. I've got no use for him.

There is one tall lady who wears the shorts and baseball hat who is my favorite delivery driver. The first time we met, she came right up to my spot at the window where I was sitting on the back of the comfy chair. I was ready to make an enemy, but she turned out to be great! She waved at me and called me a sweet baby. Then she held up the box she was holding for me to see. She left it on the porch, and when The Backup opened it up later...it was for me! I got two bags of bones and a tube of mint toothpaste! It pays to be cute, I tell you.

Like I said before, I like surprises, but sometimes a girl wants what a girl wants. I need to work on improving my powers so that the delivery drivers will not only bring me something, but something in particular if I choose...like ice cream.

Special sundae

A favorite memory of mine is when we had sundaes on a Sunday. (Using the same word two different ways. Smart and beautiful, I amaze myself.) One day out of nowhere The Backup suggested that we go for a walk across the bridge and get ice cream. Mama agreed that it was a pretty day, and a great time to go. Peanut, of course, was just all over herself, positively drooling at the idea of getting a little stray ice cream. We all know that The Backup tends to drop things, so even though she had never had ice cream, she was sure that she was about to get something fantastic.

I was a little less excited. I like walks, but this sounded like a different kind of walk. Maybe one where there would be a lot of people and dogs around. I don't like all the attention I get when we're out in public. You know, being a one person dog, and not a dog dog. Well, who am I to spoil everyone's fun?

We got in the car, and thankfully The Backup drove so I could sit in Mama's lap. I now knew for sure that I had trained them successfully. I smiled and stretched to get my nose as close to the air vent as possible. I'm no hound, but I can smell some things. The dogwoods and redbuds were just blooming, and smelled fantastic. The second sniff told me that shaggy cat had been in the yard within the last hour. That threatened to get me worked up, but I decided not to let anything ruin the day's adventure.

Pretty soon we stopped and got out of the car, then went down a sidewalk to the bridge. As soon as I set paw on that sidewalk, I could feel dozens of eyes on me. I used to worry about getting stepped on because of my small size, but when I realized that every person and every dog watches me, I traded one problem for another. What's a dog to do? I just focus on staying close to Mama, and if I really panic, I give her the look and she picks me up. I managed to walk on my own the whole trip that day.

The sidewalk ran in front of a few stores, and I insisted on being as close to the stores as possible. That way I would draw less attention, and have less going on right around me. Finally we got to the bridge.

This was some bridge. It was huge with metal pieces way up in the sky and on the sides, but the part we walked on was covered with wood. And it crossed an honest to goodness river, not a creek. It would take a lot of doggy paddling to cross that river.

We stayed on the side of the bridge while we walked. While Peanut sniffed and slobbered with the dogs we passed, I looked out over the water and enjoyed feeling the wind in my fur. I thought my fur might get messy in the wind, but I looked over my shoulder and saw that every piece was staying in place. I smiled and pushed my face up to the sun. Then I heard Mama tell someone that Peanut is the friendly one, and I'm not social. I gave her a side eye out of habit. We all knew it was true, but I don't like to have it pointed out to strangers.

After a little more walking, I heard a small voice ask to pet me. I looked over because the voice was cute. It came from a little boy wearing a bowtie and glasses. Well, for a person he was little. He was pretty big compared to me. He was adorable and polite. I would make an exception and allow this pet. I looked up at Mama and gave her the OK by squinting my eyes just a little. She squatted down beside me, put her hand lightly on my neck (I guess just in case I changed my mind), and told him he could pet my side. He gave me one soft stroke going with the grain of my fur, said thank you, and walked away. A dog would be lucky to have that boy as their person.

Soon we had crossed the bridge and gotten to the ice cream shop. This was a magical place. I saw a big plastic pony by the door, and beside the pony...a water bowl! Peanut and I went for it. We had gotten thirsty after all that walking. I hoped it wasn't river water, because I prefer filtered water, but it was so good and cold that I didn't care.

Then The Backup handed Mama Peanut's leash (I always walk with Mama, and Peanut always walks with The Backup), and went inside to get the ice cream. After we had had enough water, Mama took us to a table while we waited.

When The Backup came out, he had three saucers. Three? There were only two of them. Maybe they were extra hungry. Then he did a crazy thing and put one of the saucers on the ground. On the saucer was one of the most beautiful things I had ever seen. There were pieces of banana, globs of peanut butter, and a mound of what I guess is ice cream. I barely got a good look at it before Peanut shoved her big ugly head in it.

I wasn't about to miss out on this, so I got right in there myself. I heard people laughing smiley laughs, and somebody even clapped. I tried to use good manners, especially since we were in public, but this stuff was slap your mama good! Don't worry, I've never slapped anyone, it's just a saying. I would never slap Mama.

Head butting Beau was as violent as I've ever been.

As an extra bonus, Peanut got what Mama and The Backup called a brain freeze. This happens if you eat or drink too much cold stuff too fast. The peanut butter and bananas weren't cold, but the ice cream sure was. And Peanut has never been known to eat slowly. I think the brain freeze must have hurt, because she squeezed her eyes shut, scrunched up her face, and pulled her head back like a turtle going into its shell. The people around us stopped laughing, and acted like they felt sorry for her. I thought it was funny to watch, but I'm glad it didn't last very long, or I would have had to feel guilty for enjoying it.

Pretty soon, she perked up, and Peanut and I were pushing the saucer across the pavement trying to get every last bit of goodness in our mouths. We finally decided there was nothing left, and plopped down on the pavement to enjoy our food high. Well, really, I decided before Peanut, who actually wound up flipping the whole saucer over on top of herself in her craziness. Mama and The Backup couldn't help but laugh at that along with me. Then they ate their saucers of goodness, and we walked back to the car. It was a great day, the likes of which ordinary dogs rarely experience.

Drowning in dough?

I've never been one to brag, so this is a tough topic for me. A tell-all book, though, requires some real telling, even the uncomfortable kind. Honestly, I think that's what will make my story believable and something anyone can relate to. If everything I say is rainbows and unicorns, you will feel that I'm hiding something. And of course, it wouldn't be the truth. So I want to be transparent for all of you, my extra special audience.

I think we all know that I'm super talented. If you didn't know before you started reading this book, you do by now. If you want more proof, just wait until my picture and the paparazzi footage "leaks". There won't be any doubt then about my top level talent. Anyway, I cut off my career just when most people would say I was about to become wildly successful. What possessed me to do that?

If I had really tried, I probably could have made my way to Nashville and stardom. No, there's no doubt that I would have. I could have had the swooning fans, the houses full of flowers and gifts, and a piggy bank that regularly exploded from overfeeding. In some ways, what happened to me when I left Podunkville was just a string of bad luck. I don't believe in bad luck, or luck at all, really. It seems to me that we all get what we deserve in the end. I now think that what I needed all along was love and a real home. And Mama needed me. I know I got what I needed, I'm sure about it, because now I'm happy instead of just dreaming about being happy.

I call happiness success. And if that's true, I have buckets of success. Boatloads of success. I'm doing fine as frog's hair. You get my point. I found my place in the world, and I'm bound and determined to live in it and enjoy it as long as possible.

I'm very famous in my family and neighborhood. Once my picture makes its way around the internet, I'll probably be famous around the world, but for sure nationally. You saw my picture on the cover, right? Back in the day, this worldwide fame would have been the answer to all my prayers. Not now. It's still flattering to think that I'll be so popular, but it won't give me a fat head. I won't change myself or my life one bit, no matter how famous I get. I'll always just be sweet, adorable, humble Khaki.

Fame by itself doesn't bring lots of money. You still have to work for it, and I'm not willing to. The offers of albums, commercials, and photo shoots will all be left unanswered so I can stay in the place it took so long for me to find. This is my real work and my real treasure. A different kind of rich maybe than you expected. A better one, I think. I don't have a trust fund, credit card, or bank account. I don't even have a stash of treats buried in the backyard. I've never made a cent on my singing. It's not about fame and fortune anyway, it's about bringing joy to myself and those around me.

Mama and The Backup take very good care of me, and I trust them to keep it up. They know they have a good thing. I know it, too. I have plenty of good kibble, multiple beds, two doggy doors, and a small but on point wardrobe. I also have my person, Mama, a backup person (See how I got the name?) for when my person isn't at home, and for comic relief, I have Peanut. I have a lot of freedom, and I get a lot of lovins. Probably even a little more than I deserve, but just a smidge. What else could a girl want?

Fantastic food

I admit that I'm something of a foodie. Having no skill in the culinary area, I don't cook. I wouldn't even know which end of a whisk to use. I'm pretty sure I couldn't even if I did know. Leave that to the professionals, I say. I wouldn't call my tastes snobby, but I do have a sensitive palate. I'm thankful for what I have and will eat what I'm given with very few exceptions (I just can't make myself do spinach), but I do appreciate and enjoy the good stuff. By good stuff,

I mean the stuff that makes you lick your chops when you're finished and then dream about it when you fall asleep. Unless you daydream, then maybe you daydream about it, too.

There are two meals a day at home, because my little belly can't hold enough at one time to get me through the whole day. It's kind of like how hummingbirds have to drink nectar or sugar water all the time because they're so tiny. When I wake up in the morning, breakfast, which includes a vitamin and pumpkin, is ready for me and Peanut. I insist that Mama or The Backup be in the room while I eat. Eating alone, or even alone with Peanut, is just sad. Usually, Mama gives us our food and then eats her breakfast in the kitchen with us. She eats at the counter, but that's close enough. I don't expect her to eat out of a bowl on the floor, but it would be great if she tried it once. It would make a nice picture for a magazine article about how cool our pack family is.

I eat in a way that some might call strange, but I call it methodical and part of the comforting routine of eating. I eat in straight lines back and forth across the bowl. If anyone tells you otherwise, they are a liar and not to be trusted. I do not have OCD because one key word, obsessive, does not apply to me. I'm a creature of habit, not compulsion. So I guess that's two words that don't apply to me.

I'm going to tell you now about one of my few weaknesses. I mentioned pumpkin earlier. A while back, Mama started giving me and Peanut each a spoonful of pureed pumpkin with breakfast. Now I'm hooked, absolutely addicted! Mama said something about the pumpkin keeping me from scooting on the floor, but I don't care about that. It's delicious! Hm, maybe I should start scooting more just to get more pumpkin. Anyway, I prefer to lick it off a spoon like a civilized dog, but you better believe I'll clean my bowl if someone is thoughtless enough to drop it in there. Don't tell anyone, but I would probably even go to the groomer and calmly have my nails done if it meant a cup of pumpkin would appear in my near future. I can compromise when I have to.

For some reason I will never understand, Peanut and I share a water bowl. When she manages to get grass in the water yet again, I seriously think about having a hissy fit, but since the water bowl stays on my placemat, I try not to complain.

Speaking of my placemat, I love my placemat. It's Chihuahua chic, meaning classy and festive. It's red and covered in sombreros, maracas, and cactuses, cactuseses...cacti... maybe? I don't know, I hate English. Anyway, it's perfect for me, and much better than Peanut's placemat that's gray and has <u>Stay Pawsitive</u> written on it in cursive. At least that's what Mama said it says. And she always tells the truth.

Second food is supposed to be at 3:00. The Backup has a habit of forgetting, though, so on days when Mama is at work, I make sure to start reminding him at 2:45. I do this by stretching against his leg and flashing him my irresistible puppy dog eyes. I don't remind Mama because she's good about being on time and if she's a little late, well, you make allowances for those you love.

First we get our appetizer bones in the kitchen. Mine is smaller than Peanut's, but I don't get upset because I know this is so it won't hurt my dainty little mouth. I take it to the couch and eat it there, since I've always enjoyed changing scenery during meals. Then I hurry back to my bowl (just in case Peanut feels like "forgetting" which bowl is hers) to dig into the main course. It's the same kibble as at breakfast, but I like it: turkey and sweet potato. Perfectly balanced flavors, in my opinion. It's like Thanksgiving twice a day everyday, but I don't need stretchy pants. I really should find out who makes the kibble and have Mama send them a thank you note. That's a note I'd be happy to put my Spot Hancock on.

The Backup will let us lick his plate when he's finished eating if there's nothing we're allergic to on it. Mama doesn't like this practice, says it teaches us bad habits, and never shares her plate. She is convinced that there's no straightening The Backup out, so she just lets him do what he wants, but she looks at him kind of crazy. This is the one case where I have to disagree with Mama. She makes some tasty food, and the leftover bits on The Backup's plate are the only way I get to try it. This is the main way I get to expand my food horizons. It's hard to be a foodie if you only get one kind of kibble. The best thing I've tried was when she made blueberry cobbler. It was about as good as the special sundae, and I didn't have to worry about a brain freeze or walk through a bunch of people to get it. As expected, I will take a couple of swipes across the plate when offered, but Peanut will keep going until she licks the design off of it. She has no manners at all, that one.

In Mama's defense, she does sometimes give us something a little special to eat. If she is cooking with eggs, she might give us some yolk. This is why I come running when I hear an egg crack, just to remind her that this is something she says is OK for us to have. I'm not sure Peanut understands the effort I go to in securing us goodies. There is also the occasional milk or yogurt, again only when she is cooking. These are all things she thinks are good for us, but what I know is that they're good for my tastebuds.

The absolute best treat is when Mama and The Backup come home with a little white box filled with rib bones. This probably only happens about twice a year, but when it does, Peanut and I each get a bone for a couple of days. Not the appetizer bones, the real bones. The Backup approves because he tries to buy our love, and Mama approves because she thinks that if we get the bones just every once in a while it's good for our teeth. I don't really care about their reasoning, I just take advantage when it works to my benefit.

The fat files

I know this is going to come up at some point, so I might as well get it over with now. It's one of those skeletons I have to pull out of my closet.

There are some pictures of me, even worse than the striped sweater pictures, that could very well come out into the public eye after I go viral. I understand why they were taken, but I sure wish they had been deleted. Now it's too late.

All celebrities have fat pictures out there somewhere, and so do I. I have never been fat. I've already told you that at my size, it would be unhealthy and dangerous to get heavy. I have never been above eleven and a half pounds. I sure look fat in those pictures, though. Let me explain why those pictures are deceiving.

One day when I went on a walk with Mama, I felt a little sting on my muzzle, but it wasn't much, so I didn't make a big to-do about it. When we got home, Mama sat in the comfy chair to read a book, and I relaxed on her lap. After a few minutes, I did begin to feel a little bit of a headache starting. Still, not a big thing, so I didn't make a fuss. Soon after that, Mama looked down at me and sucked her breath through her teeth. That was when I thought about getting worried.

She grabbed me and rushed with me across the house to The Backup. She asked him if my face looked swollen. He cocked his head this way and that, closed one eye, then said he thought maybe it did. So they decided to take a picture of my face, take another one in a couple of minutes, and see if I was swollen or if it was all in their heads. Well, after the second picture, they could see that not only was I swollen, but that I was getting more swollen with time.

I had never seen Mama so worried, and she's usually a very calm person. So that's when I joined in and started worrying, too. I kept up a good front, though. I didn't whimper or thump my tail at all. She said I was allergic to something, but she didn't know what. Well, that sting on my muzzle must have had something to do with it. I would have said something when it happened if I had known it would become a problem. Now I had a swollen muzzle, a headache, and a guilty conscience. I hated that maybe I could have stopped all this drama before it started.

Mama was worrying that if it got worse I might not be able to breathe. She said that she knew dogs were given a special kind of medicine if they had problems with allergies, especially if they were swelling, and she was worried there might not be time to get me to the vet. She and The Backup both went crazy searching on their phones about this. They agreed after finding a few things that I could have a piece of a pink pill. This was supposed to keep me from swelling any more and make my muzzle go back to its normal size. Well, Mama tore up the bathroom looking for the pink pills, but she found one for me and cut it down to the right amount.

After I took the pill (it tasted like squashed grasshopper), she kept taking pictures every couple of minutes so she could compare them and see if it was working. It did. My muzzle went back to its pretty, delicate, normal state. I hadn't had the smallest bit of trouble breathing through my swollen face. My headache even went away. Mama and The Backup had saved the day!

Now we have a different problem. Between the two of them, they probably took over two dozen pictures of me with what looks like a really fat face. And those pictures were all just of my face. They tried to keep them the same so they could see changes before and after the pill. It would have been better if all of me had been in the pictures, because my body stayed the same small size as always. So now that I'm not worried about breathing anymore, I'm worried about someone dragging me through the mud. Not real mud. Some mean sneak might try to say that I had a fat phase, then had surgery to lose weight. Or they could say I had a filler explosion, or something crazy like that. I hate to even think about it.

But what's so bad about being big? It would be bad for me, but not all dogs are made the same. Sometimes things just happen. Sometimes a dog might get sad if their person left them home alone, bought a cat, or washed their favorite blanket. That kind of trauma can make a dog eat too much. Comfort kibble, we call it. A dog could also have a health problem that makes them get heavier. Like a problem with the thyroid - that's a bowtie inside the neck. It's just not anyone's place to say what size a dog should be unless they are specially qualified.

In my case, though, I was swollen, not heavy. Ugh, I don't even have a vet bill to prove my story because it was all handled at home. This is the one time I wish that Mama and The Backup were dummies. Now it will be my word against who knows how many others. I don't like the sound of that. In real life, nobody roots for the underdog. They're more worried about making money, and scandal sells. I think I'm going to have to go to bed. I've suddenly got another headache.

Bedtime rules

Bedtime is a ritual at my house, as I think it should be for all humans and dogs. Studies show that having a nighttime routine helps your brain and body get ready for sleep, so you end up sleeping better than you would if you went to sleep when and where the mood happened to strike you. I haven't actually read those studies, of course, but that's what I hear. And it makes sense to me. Basically, that's how I attack everything in life. I do what makes sense to me, because I'm no idiot.

If I learn new information, I can change, but only if it makes sense.

Most nights at our house, we all end up on the couch relaxing together. By we, I mean Mama, The Backup, Peanut and yours truly. Let me rewind a little. On days that Mama works, she has a definite routine. She comes home, eats a little something and then takes a shower. She then puts on pajamas, usually one of her three sets of llama pajamas. She thinks llamas are almost as cute as me, but at least I don't spit. Anyway, the pajamas mean that the bedtime process has officially begun. She gets a cup of tea, and we all pile on the couch to snuggle and read or watch videos on the internet. Well, Peanut and I really only participate in the snuggles unless it's an extra good video, but you know what I'm saying.

Actually, I do watch some videos because there is a series that features a dog I have a lot in common with. I don't want to name drop, because even though we've never actually met, I think of him as a friend and colleague. I'll just say this: he is a medium sized black dog who is named after a big U.S. city, and he lives across the ocean. Based on the knowledge of travel and the ocean I picked up while on vacation, that means he's somewhere on the other side of Florida. He appears in almost every video his person makes. He hasn't let all the fame get to him, though, and I admire that. Mostly, he seems bored with it all, but a lot of times he sticks his tongue out at the audience. That makes me smile every time.

After a bit of relaxing, the actual going to bed process starts. Don't get confused, this is different from the bedtime routine. From this point, the routine is the same every day, not just work days. The first cue is that Mama goes to the bathroom to work on her face. She has a much more complicated beauty routine than I do. She washes her face which requires a headband that she has to dig out of a drawer. Then she gets some kind of chemical out of a squeezy lab bottle and rubs it in her skin. Next, she has to brush her teeth and put some cream on her face. I've noticed that there are two creams, and they are each used every other night. I don't think it's a perfect system, because sometimes I hear her asking herself which one she used the day before. She talks to herself a lot. Anyway, this all happens while I'm doing some very important work. I'm a very devoted dog.

You see, when Mama goes to wash her face, I run and jump in the bed to warm it up for her. Actually, I jump <u>on</u> the bed, but I quickly work my way under the covers so I can make it nice and toasty for her. She always stays so cold. She's skinny and doesn't have much insulation. I don't have much insulation either, but I've got something even better that's both functional and beautiful. Fur. I bet she wishes she had a fur coat like me. Since she doesn't have one, I try my best to have the bed warm before she gets in. It's the only time I wish I was bigger, because I could be a more effective bed warmer.

There are two acceptable places for me once Mama gets in bed: against the small of her back, or behind her knees. Well, sometimes she warms her feet up on me, but lately she's started to wear socks to bed. This has worked out well for all of us. I'm thankful for those socks so I can spend more time in the spots I like, and she can have two warm spots at once. It goes without saying that I must remain covered under the sheet and comforter all night. If Mama is hugging The Backup, or even worse, Peanut, I have no choice but to walk over them until space is made for me between them, and this time, my two acceptable spots don't matter. I'll slide in wherever I can. Forgive me, but I have to stop and rant a bit here.

Now, I know without a doubt that Peanut is scared of thunder. Lots of dogs are. I'm not one of them because I know it's just noise, but I can understand how it could be scary. Here's the problem: I think

Peanut takes advantage of the situation. I've noticed lately that she has started to shiver if she sees heat lightning, or if it's raining hard. She will even start to drool big rivers, just for effect. Of course, Mama and The Backup are good hearted and want to make her feel better. But somehow it's not good enough when her person holds her like a human thunder shirt. Nope, she will crawl out of The Backup's arms after a couple of minutes and plunk herself down, shaking and drooling like a hot mess, right up on my person, Mama. I call this manipulation of the worst kind, not to mention that it takes away from the all important Mama and Khaki time. This seems to happen mostly at night, which is the worst time as far as I'm concerned. Night is what got me side tracked. I hadn't even meant to talk about that. Sorry.

Anyway, the point here is that we sleep as a pack, and I make sure that my place in that pack is a comfortable one next to my person.

Snoring

I'm just going to come right out and acknowledge, although it hurts my heart, that I've been accused of snoring. No one is brave enough to accuse me to my face, so obviously it's a lie that comes from either jealousy or pettiness. I always hear the rumor second or third hand. Anyway, who would spread such filthy lies about little old me I just can't imagine. If it wasn't beneath me, I would be downright angry.
Let me put this absurd idea to bed.

(An impressive word play, right?) I do not snore. I am a vocal dreamer.

You see, I have very vivid dreams. Like the best movie you've ever seen. I also dream constantly. Only when I'm asleep, though. I never daydream. Well, it doesn't seem that I can sleep at all without dreaming. That's a classic sign of a creative mind, I hear, the brain working so hard like that. Since I have so many dreams, they are of all kinds.

The good dreams are usually of me on stage singing to a sold out crowd of admiring fans or walking with Mama down a beautiful street in a highly sophisticated city. In the first case, I'm obviously performing my heart out, hitting every note perfectly, dancing better than a butterfly with tap shoes, and telling my sold-out audience how much I love them. In the second case, in keeping with good manners, I have to greet every dog and human we pass with a hello and a slight dip of my cute little apple head. Thankfully, Dogspeak is universal, so I'm understood no matter what city we happen to be in.

My favorite one of these dreams, though, is when we're in London. I'm always wearing an absolutely beautiful hat in London, usually one with a velvet ribbon to set off the white diamond on my forehead, and it makes me look like the high class lady I am.

I also have a recurring bad dream. It's terrible, but I guess it's part of my life for now. In this one, my father comes to my front door all hangdog and muddy, asking me to take him in. Well, as any sane dog would, I don't even let him set one dirty paw in the house. Can you even imagine the nerve he has, begging from a dog he treated so badly? Instead of showing him the mercy he hopes for, I tell him off for abandoning his family. I probably get a little carried away and preachy at this point. I do tend to fly off the handle when I know I'm right. We all have our faults.

At least I don't have Mama's recurring bad dream. It's a different story each time, but the end is always the same. Her teeth fall out. She tells a funny story at a friend's house, her teeth fall out. She stands in the checkout line at the grocery store, her teeth fall out. She gets a sunburn at the beach, her teeth fall out. So weird. I wouldn't be able to show my face if my teeth fell out, much less sing without projecting my voice over my megaphone teeth, so I'm hoping that my brain decides to stick with the telling-off-my-deadbeat-father dream.

There are times when I have dreams that aren't good or bad. These are about things that are happening in real life. I guess it's my way of mentally preparing myself for what I have to do when I'm awake. See, my brain works even when I'm asleep. Pretty cool, huh? I rehash therapy sessions, sometimes for a few naps afterward, letting my mind soak up all the goodness I heard but didn't quite understand at the time. If I know that an awkward situation is coming up, like when I had to tell my sister Thwerpa that she had chosen an absolutely atrocious bandana to wear on her first date with Pablo from down the road, I end up practicing in my dreams. (In case you're wondering, it was striped, <u>and</u> had polka dots. It made her look like every last bit of her spunk had been sucked out.) None of this mental work is done on purpose, it's a gift.

As you can see, all of these dreams involve me using my voice in some way. I'm not a slacker. I actively participate in my dreams, even though I don't actually choose to. I think it makes me a better dog: preparing me to beat my challenges and conquer my goals. You've been around dogs that run and kick in their sleep. They're dreaming about playing fetch and chasing squirrels. I talk and sing in my sleep because I'm dreaming big, next level dreams. So, I'm a vocal dreamer, not a snorer like some might say. Only common dogs snore. The kind of dog that slurps their water and eats anything that isn't nailed down. I am not one of those dogs.

The Running of the Chihuahuas

In my new forever hometown, they have an amazing tradition called, get this now it's beautiful, The Running of the Chihuahuas. This happens when two very special days somehow happen on the same day. Lots of special happening, right? Those days are Cinco de Mayo and the Kentucky Derby. Cinco de Mayo is a Mexican holiday, and the Kentucky Derby is a yearly big fancy race for horses in, you guessed it, Kentucky.

I have a very unique connection to both of those days, and they are extra important to me. Maybe you didn't know this, but way back when, Chihuahuas came from Mexico. And here's a super cool fact: they even named a state in Mexico after us sweet little dogs. My tie to Kentucky is that Mama has family living there. I think she might even be from there. Yes, she says that she and The Backup are both from Kentucky. So you can see how a one of a kind event like The Running of the Chihuahuas, which happens to combine both of these special places, would be almost magical for me.

Chihuahuas from all over come to run in this race. The winner gets a little Chihuahua-sized golden sombrero, which is a type of Mexican hat, and in this case, a major piece of bling. Let me tell you about when I won that race, well, it was the only time I ran in it. I won't run again, because that would be unfair to the other Chihuahuas. Besides, this one time was so amazing that I don't need to repeat it.

I know what you're thinking. I've made it pretty clear that I'm not into exercise or sweat. In general, you're right. A little glistening during a performance is acceptable, but that's the only time. Other than that, I'm not going to do any exercise that isn't part of being a normal happy dog. Well, I'm not athletic, but I like to win important things, and I <u>wanted</u> that sombrero.

I won that race without even training. Work smarter, not harder, you know. The key was knowing what I was getting myself into. I did some asking around, a kind of friendly and effective research, and found out everything I needed to know. The race is held in a huge building where twenty Chihuahuas can run at the same time. Hundreds of people come to watch and root for their favorite runner, many wearing fancy hats and drinking mint juleps. (I don't think the hats and juleps mattered much, but I thought I'd tell you everything I learned, just in case.) Each Chihuahua has two people, one at the starting line, and one at the finish line. The race itself is very simple. When the bell rings, the starting line person lets go of their runner. The Chihuahua runs to the finishing line person. The fastest is the winner, and gets an amazing sombrero.

All I really needed to do to win this thing was focus. I didn't need to be the fastest. I just needed to tune out all the distractions. I was sure that most of the dogs wouldn't even make it to the finish line, and I was right.

The day of the race, I admit that I only ate half my breakfast, partly because I was a little nervous, and partly because I didn't want all that kibble slowing me down. Mama and The Backup quickly and correctly decided that he should be at the starting line and I would run to Mama. That was a no brainer. I felt confident because I had no reason not to feel that way. I'm great at everything, so why not winning races too?

Even though I knew what was coming, I was shocked when we got there. It was <u>really</u> loud. I was wishing for doggy ear plugs, but I'm not sure they even exist. I'm going to have to look into that.

I was registered, and got to wear my favorite number, 7. I did look good with that number 7 tag on my chest, like a cute furry marathon runner. I had thought about asking for a sweatband before the race, but decided against it since it would cover up the pretty diamond on my forehead. I wanted my winner's circle picture to be perfect. As I expected, there was a dog on both sides of me. Well, lots of dogs on both sides of me. It was a full race of twenty Chihuahuas. I use the word Chihuahua loosely.

You know I'm only half Chihuahua, and it seems that a lot of the other dogs were only part Chihuahua, too. I saw other apple heads and some deer heads, some with long legs that could have pulled off cowboy boots, some with spots on their fur. One was even brindle. I was one of the bigger dogs, which is something I'm not used to.

Once we got to the starting line, I started preparing myself for the bell. See, it's easy to get scared by a noise like that and forget what you're supposed to do. Like a deer (head) in headlights, they say. I couldn't do that and have a chance at winning, so I just wouldn't do that. Simple plans are usually the best.

Then all at once, the people at both ends of the racetrack squatted down. The Backup and all the people on our end had their hands around their runners. Most of the runners looked as nervous as turkeys in November. Then the bell dinged, everyone let go, and the craziness started. I'm not going to lie, I was almost ashamed to be part Chihuahua after I saw how those dogs acted.

Some of the runners never even moved. They were too scared. They just stood there, shaking in their sneakers. I don't think any of us were wearing shoes, but you know what I'm saying. Well, I took off and started on the next part of my strategy, singing one of my songs to myself so I could block out the noise and stay focused on Mama at the finish line. Let me tell you, the crowd was going wild.

People were yelling and whistling, clapping and laughing like you could only understand if you've been to a Chihuahua race. This freaked out a lot of the runners, and a few left the racetrack and ran into the crowd trying to escape. One poor long haired Chihuahua made it halfway to the finish, then stopped and piddled out of sheer terror. From the corner of my eye, I saw another one running in tight little circles like she was touched in the head. When I was almost to Mama, I decided to chance looking around me. There was only one other dog still in the race. And it looked like he was going to beat me. Well, I couldn't have that. There was a golden sombrero on the line, not to mention all the glory and bragging rights.

I had to do something, and I didn't have much time to make a decision. I'm a little embarrassed by what I did next, but it was worth it. I used my irresistible charms on a helpless boy. I barked at him in my sweetest voice, called him big boy even though I probably had three pounds on him, and asked him to wait for me. Would you believe that he did? The goober actually slowed down, and with a wink, I pranced right past him into Mama's arms.

Ah, victory. So good. Almost as good as I look in that golden sombrero.

Question & Answer time

Every time I have shared my story with people, they just gushed about it. That's why I felt that I had to put the reviews at the front of this book. They also had some questions for me that weren't quite going to fit into what I have had Mama write down. So I've decided to include this small Q&A section to cover what they asked me, and also what I think others might like to ask me if they had the chance.

Why didn't you share your amazing story with us before?
I would have to say that my modesty and a life full of changes held me back. I'm settled enough now to collect my thoughts, and with the threat of the media invading my privacy, I really had no choice.

You are incredibly eloquent. What kind of education do you have?
Thanks. I am a self-made dog. I have zero formal education. It just wasn't necessary. I've done my best to watch those around me and learn from what I saw. And of course, those who have been a big

part of my life have influenced me, especially my mother, Aarfah, Mama, and The Backup. They are all very intelligent.

If you could have lunch with any dog, who would it be?
There are so many amazing dogs, I don't think I can pick just one. I would have to say a therapy dog, though. Their huge hearts and brains have my respect.

What about a historical person? Who would you choose for lunch?
Mozart. He made some amazing music, so we have something in common. I think he also had a reputation for being kind of crazy, so I'd like to know what that looks

like. I would need Mama there as my Dogspeak translator, of course.

Mozart spoke German. Does your Mama know German? How would you address that?
German? You mean there is more than one people language? What a shame. Next question.

Are there any potential boyfriends out there?
I could jerk a knot in your tail. We've already talked about this. I like to look, and that's it.

If you could buy any one thing, what would you choose?
Hmm...that's a bit tricky. Oh, I got it! I would buy a giant doggy sundae and take it to the jail I did

time in so all the inmates could share it.

What law would you like to see passed?
I mentioned in the book how not being allowed in most restaurants just flies all over me. I would like to see a law passed that any dog is allowed in any public place, including restaurants, parks, stores, and offices.

Where do you see yourself in five years?
In Mama's lap.

What's your favorite color?
I don't really have any way to answer that unfair question. Dogs

are mostly color blind. Didn't you know that? Bless your heart.

Oops. What's your favorite season?
I love the fall. It's so much fun to walk on all those crunchy leaves, and I get to sniff them too. It's the only time of year I get to know what it smells like up in the top of a tree.

If you could be anything other than a dog, what would you choose?
Well, if you can't be the best thing in the world, be the second best. A butterfly. They fly. And smell flowers. Enough said.

What do you consider your greatest accomplishment?

I once wrote an entire song in fifteen minutes flat. Also, I make someone smile every day.

Finishing Remarks

Thank you for reading my exclusive tell-all book. I just know you loved it! It's been so much fun working on this book, even though it's been a lot of hard work. I've gotten to spend a whole lot of quality time with Mama telling her my thoughts, and I'm looking forward to seeing our finished product soon. And, thankfully, it seems that my story will be out before the paparazzi and tabloids invent their own twisted version of me. I guess staring down that teenager who took my picture bought me enough time to do what I had to do. So there, beanie boy!

I hope that you've come to understand that while I might be an exceptional dog, I'm really just like everyone else, but with a few exceptions. I usually prefer to speak in my own words, but I would like to share an especially touching and inspirational quote as I wrap this thing up. I'm sure you will find it as moving as I did.

> *Most adventures start with a dumb idea and*
> *an unreasonable amount of determination.*

Now I have a favor to ask you. Recommend this book to as many friends as you can so the truth about me goes out faster than the media can do their evil work of tearing me down. Now that I think about it, I wouldn't mind if you recommended the book to enemies and strangers, too. Mind you, this isn't about fame. I happily let go of that dream when I met my person, my Mama, but it *is* about protecting my reputation. That is after all, my most valuable possession besides my Christmas sweater.

If you have learned anything, maybe from the fashion or hygiene chapters, please feel free to imitate me. I would find that to be a great complement. I love the idea of improving a life.

Lots of tail wags and snuggles,
Khaki

Thanks for reading my fun little book! If you enjoyed it, or were even slightly amused, I would appreciate a review on Amazon or a recommendation to a friend.

About the Authors:

Anne Compton is an LPN who prefers daydreaming and writing to actual work. Her other interests include baking, history, and anything related to travel.

Khaki has filled an entire small book with her delusions of grandeur. No other information is available, but you've probably had enough anyway.

Also by Anne Compton:

*In the House of Schizophrenia: A Certifiable Memoir

*The Healing Sin (historical fiction)

*Staying Home:
A Practical Guide to Promoting Independence

*Home Again:
Finding the Best Placement when Home isn't an Option

Made in United States
North Haven, CT
08 September 2025